MYRNA MACKENZIE

MYRNA MACKENZIE

is a winner of the Holt Medallion honoring outstanding fiction and she was a finalist for numerous other awards, including the Orange Rose, the National Reader's Choice Awards, the *Romantic Times* Reviewers Choice and WisRWA's Write Touch. A former teacher and college recruiter, she loves trying new things and has had many hobbies in addition to reading, her first and favorite. Others include gardening (despite a brown thumb), needlework, travel, camping, hiking (despite the occasional bear), collecting cookbooks she rarely uses and thinking up new ways to avoid housework.

Mackenzie resides in the Chicago suburbs with her husband and two teenage sons, and her current favorite hobby is being an avid cross country/track and field cheerleader, at which she excels (all it takes is a good set of lungs and an excess of enthusiasm). Readers may visit her at her Web site at www.myrnamackenzie.com or write to her at P.O. Box 225, LaGrange, IL 60525.

MORNING BEAUTY, MIDNIGHT BEAST

MYRNA MACKENZIE

Silhouette *Books*

Published by Silhouette Books
America's Publisher of Contemporary Romance

SILHOUETTE BOOKS

MORNING BEAUTY, MIDNIGHT BEAST

ISBN 0-373-21851-6

Visit Silhouette Books at www.eHarlequin.com

Printed in U.S.A.

Chapter 1

Molly gritted her teeth against the pain that started low in her back and swelled outward. Again. This was the third time since she'd started home. But it was nothing. It couldn't be time yet. She was only eight months along. Besides, she had heard about such things, pain that started and faded away. A lie, a trick of the system. The fact was that she had just spent too much time on her feet today, and the discomfort would stop soon for sure. Besides, she was still four blocks from home. Nothing to do but keep on walking.

"Everything is going to turn out fine, Ruthie Ann. It will," she promised, smoothing one hand over the mass of her abdomen and clutching her slippery packages with her other arm as she shuffled forward. "Let Mom tell you about all the pretty lights and decorations I saw today, and when we get home I'll put up our tree. It's small, angel. A sweet little thing. Like you. But it's plenty big for the two of us. You'll see when you finally get out and can look for yourself."

She tried to smile as the aching web of distress within her grew stronger, stealing her breath this time. The sidewalk stretched out in a narrow, crooked swoop of gray that was long. Very long. Home couldn't be close enough. The cold wrapped itself around her. It climbed inside her. Molly forced herself to keep shoving one foot in front of the other, to keep moving past each crack in the walkway.

"It's okay, Ruthie. We're doing okay. Keep kicking those little feet of yours, sweetie. Relax. Be calm. Maybe we'll call the doctor when we get home after all," she whispered. "Just to make sure you're all right. But of course you are. Of course you're perfectly fine." The words dropped low and fast as she tried to increase her pace.

The dark was deeper here, the lights that illuminated the shopping area blocks back more sparse. Long stretches of vision-stealing shadow were broken only by the brilliant biting glare of the street corners. And the next corner was coming up, but slowly. So slowly. The pressure in her back spread in long, unstoppable waves. It moved much faster than her feet.

She should have started back sooner, but it was Christmas, and she wanted everything to be ready for her baby. She wanted life to be perfect the way it hadn't been for her.

"Almost home, sweetheart." She gasped out the words on a breath as the pain receded and she inched her way to the corner, across the street, and up the next.

"Almost there," she said again as she felt it coming back, chasing her down. The pain had fed and grown this time. It threatened to take over her whole body, to swallow her child.

Lurching forward, spilling her packages, Molly felt her toe nick against the thick rise of an uneven sidewalk slab. Instinctively she raised one arm, curling the other over her stomach as the black ground came up to meet her. Moving too fast to stop herself, she twisted, trying to shield her child from the fall.

Not alone. Not this way. The words shot through her brain. Despair engulfed her. Then the ground smacked her with a mighty blow and the world exploded into great shards of light.

His eyes were accustomed to darkness, so Seth McCabe had no trouble making out the small lump of clothing and sprawled limbs blocking the walkway that led from his apartment building. A drunk or an addict, he thought at first, but he'd seen more than his share of such and this particular person didn't have that stripped-to-the-soul look.

Seth stepped closer, knelt and reached out.

"What in the—damn," he said, noting the small pool of blood beneath the beauty's matted curls, the telltale swell of advanced pregnancy beneath her too-snug coat.

Her hand was cold, the pulse faintly flickering. She shouldn't be moved, but it was freezing here, the ground obscenely so.

"Ada," he bellowed, calling for his neighbor and landlady, an ancient woman who lived in the basement.

No answer. She'd be asleep. Of course she would. Ada went to bed with the sun's last light.

"Ada," he yelled again, reaching the window in three quick strides and beating on it with his bare knuckles. "Ada, it's Seth," he yelled, when he saw the light come on and her face approaching the glass. "Call for an ambulance. There's a woman out here. Hurt. Pregnant. Very cold."

"Okay, I'm coming. I'm coming. I'll call. Be out there in a minute," the woman yelled, whisking aside the sheer curtains and motioning him back to his post.

That was all there was time for. His voice had ripped through the night and apparently through the young woman's consciousness, too. She stirred, and he rushed back, kneeling at her side.

He pulled off his jacket. Smelly. Dirty. He didn't want to let it touch her, but he couldn't leave her in the cold alone, and Ada was old. It would be long minutes before she would be able to bring him a blanket.

Carefully he tented the cloth around her, building a cocoon.

"Shh. Don't move," he whispered. "Be still. Help will be here soon and we'll get you to the hospital."

Small fingers reached out and clamped his wrist with a desperate, squeezing grip.

"My baby. Ruthie. She's coming. She's coming too soon." Her voice was rushed, pain-drenched, scared.

"Don't let me—not here on the ground. It's so cold. Too cold for her," she begged.

Seth felt rather than saw her head bobbing back and forth in denial.

He brushed a dirty finger across the smoothness of her cheek, trying to get her to lie still. "Don't do that, lady. You may have injured your back or your neck. When the paramedics come, we'll move you somewhere warm. Until then, blankets are on the way," he soothed. "We'll take care of you."

But her moan of denial was almost animal-like. "No." She planted her hands on the ground, trying to sit up. "Not my back or neck. Just—my shoulder. I'm—fine. Got to get to the hospital now. It's too soon. Please. Please."

Those small, gripping fingers latched on to his. He felt determination in that grasp. And pain. And most of all, fear. That was it. She was probably right—and wrong, too. It wasn't just her shoulder. She'd winced when he'd touched her face. But the temperature was dropping. He had to get her out of this. If her baby was early, she might not have the luxury of waiting for rescue to arrive. Seconds could count. Half seconds. Come on, hadn't he already learned the danger of waiting when lives were at stake? Dark, aching images threatened to rise up, but he shut them down. Forced himself to fill his mind only with the moment and the woman before him.

"You got it, lady. Let's get you to help ASAP." And kneeling before her, Seth gently scooped her into his arms. He had no car, no need of one in a city like Chicago, but Ada had an ancient clunker she parked on the street, and he knew she duct-taped spare keys under the front license plate.

"I'm taking your car, and I hope you've got gas, Ada," he bellowed as the lady in question made it to the street and wrapped him and his package in white wool. "Call off the rescue team. Tell them we couldn't wait."

Depositing his passenger as carefully as he could in the back seat, Seth spun out of the tight space and roared off into the night.

"The hospital's—"

"Don't worry, lady. Been there more than a few times. Hold on, and we'll have you to help inside of five minutes." If we don't get stopped for speeding or running red lights, he thought, slowing down slightly to make sure the intersection was clear, then pushing the accelerator as far as he dared in a populated area.

There was no answer from the back seat, just a thick, struggling gasp and a muffled moan.

Damn, he hated this kind of stuff. Why couldn't someone else have found this one, someone more suited to heroics? Not him. He didn't do dead-center Samaritanism. Not anymore.

"You okay?" he asked when she still hadn't spoken.

He went through another intersection, slowing to hazard a swift glance back. The glare of streetlights reflected off a pair of night-darkened eyes and showed small teeth biting into her lip.

"Faster," she begged, sucking in air and letting out a guttural groan.

The hospital rose up on the next block, a white glow that seemed to promise safety but which Seth knew was a lie at times.

In a squeal of brakes, he screamed up to the curb, threw open his door and hers and gathered her close. Even pregnant as sin, she was nearly weightless in his arms. Tension stiffened her slender limbs, and he felt an unwelcome urge to pull her even closer, to somehow comfort.

"Come on, lady, hang on," he ordered, rushing for the emergency room doors. "Just a few more minutes and you and the kid will be tucked safely away."

Away from him. And his part would be done. Over. Finished. Great.

He skidded up to the desk.

"She's having a baby. She's early. She's hurt," he declared to the woman looking down at the papers on her desk. "She needs attention. Fast," he added.

The woman stiffened at the tone and frowned. She opened her mouth, clearly ticked off, then sucked in her breath and raised her brows as she saw who and what was in front of her.

"McCabe?" Still she hesitated, blowing out a deep breath.

"No time for that exciting insurance talk you love this time, Stace. Make it right and get whatever questions you need answered as you go, all right?"

The clerk made a quick assessment of the damaged, frantic woman in his arms, calling for the triage nurse who quickly sized up the situation and moved into action. Quietly asking questions of her patient, she asked Seth to help with the wheelchair.

Lowering the lady he'd been holding, Seth looked at her. For the first time they were face-to-face in a well-lit room, and he noted the slight, shocked widening of lovely brown eyes as she saw what stared back at him from the mirror every day.

"Thank you," she managed to whisper as he released his grip on her.

"Anyone you need me to call? You want to give me your name, and the name and number of your next of kin?"

"Molly," she said simply as another pain caught her, doubling her over. "No one." And then she was gone.

For one frozen second, the brain that protected him from totally stupid acts shut down. She looked so small, surrounded by all that metal. He wanted to follow, to ask who had gotten her pregnant and left her alone, to issue orders to the nurse to take good care of her.

But he clenched his hands and willed his mind back on to saner paths. He'd been forced to act and he had acted, but he was glad that *his* part was over. Besides, she was in good hands, Seth reminded himself. He might have a personal distaste of hospitals, a slimy mix of gratitude and loathing, but he knew that Central Chicago Community had an excellent staff. Overworked but dedicated.

She'd be fine. Of course she would. And even if she wouldn't—

"You never came in and let Dr. Knight follow up on that last knife wound, I hear, McCabe," the clerk said, her voice a reprimand as Seth walked past on his way to the door.

Automatically he raised his hand to the jagged scar that ran from his eye to his ear, one of several that crisscrossed his cheeks in addition to the waxy pink burn mark that marred the left side of his forehead.

"It's fine, Stace," he said, continuing on his way.

"We've got some talented plastic surgeons here, McCabe. Some of those scars could be smoothed out a bit. You don't have to leave them as they are."

"Builds character." He turned and faced her as if to prove his point, frowning for the best effect.

"Hmpff," was her only response to his blatant attempt to shock the socks off her. "You gonna check up on her later?"

And then what? he asked himself. They'd become pen pals? She'd feel honor-bound to send him a fruitcake every Christmas? He'd start to worry about her, to wonder how she was doing?

"You'll take good care of her. I'm done here," he said, echoing his former thoughts as he wandered back onto the street. He was used to walking away, used to doing what was necessary and then moving on, and there was still plenty of the night left to him. Time to get some work done.

But as he ditched Ada's jalopy at home and made his way to the grittier streets of the city, a pair of sad brown eyes rose before him.

He shut down his conscience, turned his attention to the homeless shifting their weight from one foot to another, trying to keep warm on a night where there was no warmth to be had. He forced himself to pay attention, to record the sounds and smells and feel of this place.

Still later as he sat at his computer, pounding the keys, the memory of a woman's softly spoken words of gratitude intruded on his thoughts and made him garble his text.

He put his headphones on and let Vivaldi drown out the echo of a voice that had been sweet even though it had been filtered through a fog of hurt.

And when he woke uncharacteristically in the dying hours of the morning, wondering what the night had brought for one small, slender woman and one child pushing her way into the world before her time had come, Seth got up and left the house and the temptation of the telephone.

He moved back into a pocket of the city where crime and ugliness had a place in the spectrum of life. Where trust was dangerous, and every man was essentially alone. By choice.

And he was home.

* * *

Molly wandered down the street for the fifth time in as many days. She held her lumpy, blanket-shrouded bundle close to her and felt Ruthie Ann's little lips touch the spot of skin where she had left her coat open so they could have contact.

"I haven't seen him yet," she whispered. "If I could only remember which house it was…but I just can't re-call. That can't matter, though, because we have to find him. We just have to be really careful while we look. I can't let the wrong person find us. We really shouldn't even be wandering the streets like this. Still, that man did save our lives that night. I think…I'm afraid that he did even more than that, and so we absolutely have to settle up with him soon. It's been more than a month. I just wish I knew who he was."

She hated that, the fact that she didn't know his name when she knew so much more: his comfort, his touch, his voice, a pair of ocean-deep gray eyes, a face like no other. His face was fierce, scarred, maybe even frightening to some. It was the kind of face a person didn't meet up with often on a city street, not during the naked lightbulb bright-ness of daytime. And that was what worried her most.

What if he stayed inside all day? The man had paid her bills. She was sure he had, judging by the hospital gossip and the guilty, evasive looks on the nurses' faces when she had asked. She couldn't have that. She could never be indebted to any man, not after that nightmare experience with her ex-fiancé, Kevin Rickman. The thought that anyone might have control over her in any way, even anonymously, and even if their paths never crossed again, was just unthinkable. It terrified her.

"We're going to find him and pay him back some-how," she promised again.

The baby blew a wet bubble against her mother's skin. When the sudden, ear-assaulting roar of an engine made Molly jump, and a choking cloud of black smoke had her coughing and trying to shield Ruthie, she turned her back to the car. Her ears caught the cadence of a sharp metallic clicking.

"That's it," she whispered, spinning around.

The ancient gray sedan meant nothing to her. Nothing fell into place when she saw it, and no bells began to ring. But that sound…over and over her in the back of her mind, she heard it. She remembered the accompanying pain as if it were still funneling through her in great, heaving waves.

Without hesitation, Molly rushed to the passenger window, rapping against the grimy glass.

Long seconds ticked by. She rapped again as the window was slowly rolled down.

"What do you want?" An iron-haired woman with hard, black marble eyes demanded.

A woman. Not the one at all.

"I—I rode in this car. I'm sure of it," Molly stammered. "The night I had my baby, but—"

"She came out all right then?" the woman growled, but her face lost some of its sternness.

Molly held Ruthie closer. She nodded. "She's perfect, but…the man—"

"What man?" The crabbiness had returned like an angry tornado.

"The one who drove me to the hospital. Does he live around here, too? Are you related?"

The woman snorted and shook her head. "Why do you care?"

"I want to thank him, to pay him back."

"Don't bother. He won't want your thanks."

She'd already figured that much. The clerk at the hospital had been every bit as secretive as this witchy woman.

"Does he live here?" Molly persisted.

But the woman was already rolling her window up. Molly pounded on the moving glass one more time. Louder.

"Stop that," the woman ordered, stalling the window one inch from the top. "Give it up, lady. Just be grateful everything turned out well. The man you're looking for doesn't really exist. As to where he lives…anywhere. Everywhere."

"Here?" Molly pointed to the apartment building closest to the car.

"Not really."

As the woman drove away, puffing smoke out the back of her car, Molly pondered her words.

"Not really, Ruthie Ann," she said. "That must mean he's here now and then, anyway. That means if we keep looking…"

It bothered her a bit that the man didn't want her thanks, but it didn't change things. She had lived much of a lifetime with other people who hadn't wanted her, either. People who had tried to control her thoughts, her actions, who had not cared a bit what she wanted or needed. Now she made her own choices, and she tried to choose what was right when it came to right and wrong. Thanking someone who had saved her life and her baby's…well, that just had to be the only right thing to do. More important, there was the matter of the money. It scared her. Clearly the man didn't want any more contact with her, but he had plunked down big-time money for her baby. That just couldn't pass. She could not be indebted to a man, especially one she knew nothing about. Money meant power, and she was never letting a man have power over her again.

Besides, she was making her own rules for living now, flying by the seat of her pants. She wasn't sure what she was doing half the time, but she was pretty darn sure that the next step in her life had to be concentrating on building a world and a nest for Ruthie. And a woman who spent as much time as she did looking over her shoulder needed to make sure that nest was safe.

Molly shivered and pulled her baby closer. She was all that Ruthie Ann had and all that her daughter could depend on. "Which means," she told her baby, "that right now you and Mom have to go to work. Later, we'll try to figure out how to locate our mystery man.

Unfortunately, he appears to be better at hiding than we are. Even so, we're going to find him. A strong, independent woman stands on her own two feet, Ruthie. She pays her debts so that she has to depend on and answer to no one. Remember that."

Ruthie Ann made a smacking sound.

"If that means, look out, mister, the Delavan women are on your trail, then I agree," Molly said. "As soon as work is over today, we're going to lay siege to this apartment building."

Chapter 2

"I saw her today."

Seth stared out the door he had just opened and gazed right into the smug look plastered on Ada's face.

"What are you doing up here, Ada?"

She crossed her arms and looked over the rims of her glasses at him. "Told you. I saw her again today."

"Saw who? Ada, I'm three stories up. No way do you have any business huffing and puffing your way up all those stairs."

"Hmpff. I'm not getting chummy with the funeral directors yet. You just don't like anyone nosing into your business."

"You're right. That's why I chose this place. I

thought any normal eighty-year-old woman would stay on her own floor."

"Must be disappointing to find out you were wrong, then."

"Must be. Especially since I've been living here three years and you've never bothered crawling up my way before."

"Never had anything to say then. Not like now."

She waited expectantly. He felt like simply letting her wait. But she *was* eighty years old, and as his landlady she had the right to demand he let her in. The fact that she hadn't done so in the past tipped the scales. Seth swung back the door to allow her past him.

Ada shook her head. "I didn't come up here to bother you. Much. I just wanted to let you know that she's still looking for you. Her and that baby."

He didn't ask who she meant. No need to, since she'd already told him several days ago, and since Stacey at the hospital had already told him the woman had been asking questions, too.

"It's not right, you letting her wander around looking for you when you're right here."

"She'll go away soon. She'll accept the fact that she's not going to find me, and the fire will die down."

"I'm not so sure about that. Not when she suspects you and I have some sort of connection. And she's starting to attract attention. No surprise with a looker like her, but I just thought you should know since you seem so hell-bent on staying in the shadows."

He looked down at the old woman then, and she stared him straight in the eye. She didn't flinch, even though he knew his face was no prize on an ordinary day, and that consternation only worsened the effect.

"So what are you suggesting, Ada?"

"I'm not suggesting anything, but if you were to let the woman get her thank-yous off her chest, things could probably settle back down around here. She seems to think she owes you gratitude, and it's bothering her that she hasn't been able to do anything about it."

"It bothers *you* that she comes around looking for me?"

Ada's iron-gray brows drew together. Her mouth pursed up, emphasizing the age lines that lived around her lips. "A woman shouldn't be wandering the streets for hours. It's not safe. It's cold. And I can't watch my TV shows when I see her feet passing by my windows again and again."

A low chuckle escaped Seth. "Ah, so it's an act of mercy you're wanting me to perform, Ada? Get rid of the woman so you can watch MacGyver reruns in peace."

Ada leaned forward, crossing her arms. "A man who wants to be left alone is a thing I can understand. A man who hides from a woman is another thing entirely."

He sucked in a deep breath. "I'm hiding, am I?"

"Looks that way to me. If you'd wanted the woman to freeze to death, you could have left her lying on the ground."

And with that, Ada turned and went back down the stairs.

"If you don't talk to her soon, McCabe, I'm going to tell her every secret I know about you."

"You don't know my secrets, Ada," he called down.

"I don't, but I could find out if I wanted to." And then the door to her apartment clicked closed behind her.

Seth was left staring at the white plaster walls and the faded rose-patterned carpeting. He frowned and moved back into his own apartment. Night was near, but he didn't turn on the lights. Instead he leaned against the wall, sliding slowly to the floor, his long legs stretched out in front of him.

Ada was right. She could easily have found out anything she wanted to know long ago, but she hadn't. She'd left him in peace, and that was the reason the two of them got along.

But this new hitch in his life, this woman scooting up and down the street, trying to find out who he was, setting up some do-gooder's mission to shake his hand and offer him thanks he didn't want or need, was an intrusion of a different kind. No doubt he shouldn't have paid the woman's hospital bill, but it was obvious as heck that she couldn't cover the costs herself. Besides…well, he had his own reasons for paying the woman's bill, retribution for things he had failed to do in the past.

Still, he couldn't have the woman coming around. He couldn't work if he had to worry about being followed, if he had to worry about protecting some innocent from wandering in where she didn't belong. And if she was tailing him, she might end up in some very deadly places. Or she might blow his cover. No one knew or could know who wrote the "Mean Streets" column for the *Chicago Standard*. There were hundreds of stories on the streets waiting to be told, but to get those stories, he had to be able to blend in, to be at home in the parts of town where no one willingly chose to go. Except for him. Because he belonged there. Because, without his work, there would be only…thought…memories…the fear that woke him up shaking and perspiring in the night.

He'd hoped the lady would have given up by now. He hadn't wanted to see her again.

"You dog. You're lying. You liked looking at her and the way her body fit into your arms, McCabe."

Yes, and he hated the fact that she'd dragged any feeling from him at all. That wasn't like him. He felt only what he allowed himself to feel, which was almost nothing. No doubt his reaction had been brought on by the fact that everything had happened so suddenly he hadn't had time to erect any fences. But none of that mattered now, and it looked like Ada was right. The beautiful lady with the big brown eyes, the soft skin and the baby was more persistent than he'd anticipated.

He had to make her go away and not come back. Now.

* * *

The man obviously didn't want to be found.

"He's avoiding us for some reason, Ruthie Ann. We need to make it clear that we're not interested in interfering in his life. But it's really important that we locate him and do what we have to do, so we can move on. I just hope it happens soon."

Molly stopped walking and looked up at the street that was starting to empty now that dusk was falling and the light was growing dim. She had lost time the past few weeks when Ruthie was too young to bring out and about, and now it was already almost February and she was coming up against one dead end after another. She spent her days as an assistant in a bakery, taking her baby with her, but that left only evenings and Sundays to search for her unknown rescuer.

"You'd think we could find one single man when we know more or less where we were that night. The man who saved us knew that woman we saw. He called her by name. He took her car. Sooner or later, he has to go back there, don't you think?"

She looked down at Ruthie, who was blowing bubbles and kicking her legs inside her baby snowsuit. Molly smiled and gathered the little body close.

"I think your mother is just going to have to be more aggressive, sweetie," she told Ruthie. "Maybe I'll have to camp out on the lady's doorstep until our unknown hero shows up."

"That wouldn't be a wise move, lady. Think again."

The strong male voice came from the shadows and Molly gasped, hugging Ruthie tightly and whirling to see who had spoken.

But she already knew the answer to that. Her midnight stranger had startled her, it was true, but she knew his voice. It was a soft, sensual voice that came upon her in dreams in the middle of the night, a voice belonging to a faceless, nameless man. Ever since that night, these dreams had come, and she woke alone in the darkness, her hands empty and reaching.

Molly frowned and stifled a groan. She supposed those sensual dreams were simply the result of her enforced solitude. At any rate, it certainly wasn't this man's fault that his voice haunted her. She hoped her face didn't reveal her thoughts.

"Why shouldn't I camp out on your friend's doorstep?" she finally asked. "It seemed the only way I might find you."

She had moved closer to him, but she still couldn't see the man, and Molly realized that he had stepped away, into the deeper darkness beneath an awning.

"You didn't need to find me. And Ada wouldn't hesitate to call the cops if she thought I had a trespasser," he said.

"She knows I've been looking for you."

"Yes. She told me you'd been here several times. She asked me to accept your thanks. I'm doing it."

The words came out slowly, stiffly, as if they were being dragged from his body.

"So…you can stop trying to find me now. You've found me. You've thanked me. You can go home now."

She raised her brows. "But I'm not done yet. I owe you more. I owe you money."

"No. You don't."

"You paid my hospital bill, didn't you?"

"Someone tell you that?"

"Not exactly. It was more the way the people at the hospital looked when I asked about it. It was obvious someone had paid, and that the same someone didn't want me to know."

"If that someone didn't want you to know, then why are you snooping?"

"Snooping?" Something hard and stubborn rose up inside Molly. "I wouldn't call it that."

"What would you call it?"

"Taking control of my life, teaching my daughter right from wrong. Taking money from strangers is wrong."

He didn't answer. So, she had finally found something he couldn't argue with.

"Make an exception in this case," he said suddenly, sending her sense of accomplishment floundering.

"I'm sorry. I can't do that."

"Sure you can." His words were casual, his voice firm. Most people would walk away now, she realized, but most people hadn't lived the life she'd lived. As a child, she'd been forced to smile for the cameras, a child star until she wasn't young and cute anymore, at which point she had been abandoned like a junk car, dumped on her aunt. Later, when both her parents and aunt had died, there had been Kevin. She'd thought he loved her, but she had been wrong. All he'd been interested in was her former fame, and worse, her child's potential to someday make bundles of money for him. He had threatened and verbally abused her and he had used very effective tools to get her to do as he wished. So, having a man tell her to go away wasn't all that frightening in the grand scheme of things. She didn't pay that much attention to what people wanted anymore, because what they wanted had seldom been in her best interests. And now she had her child's interests at stake.

"You're done hanging around here," the man insisted. "Picking you up was just a gut reaction. It was nothing."

Molly frowned. "I don't consider my life and the life of my baby to be nothing. If you hadn't come along, we might have died. I live alone. No one would have come looking for us."

Suddenly the man stepped from under the awning. His gray eyes were darker than the shadows filling in the hollows of the buildings. The pale scar on his rigid cheekbone stood out in stark relief against the skin surrounding it. He moved closer.

"Damn it, don't you even have an ounce of common sense? How do you know I'm not a stalker, that I wouldn't come to your house and take anything I wanted? Don't you know better than to tell a man that you're living alone?"

His voice was low and hard. His long dark hair swished forward with his movements, made it hard to think about anything but him.

Stop that, Molly told herself. No wonder the man wanted nothing to do with her. Those extra hormones that had been coursing through her body for months were suddenly acting up. If he even knew what had just gone through her mind...

Maybe he did. She studied the angry man before her, saw his clenched fists, the way he seemed to be fighting to control his emotions.

"This would be a real good time for you to go home," he said softly. "You shouldn't be here. Not when you don't know anything about me."

She didn't, not at all, and yet...

"You wouldn't hurt us," she said suddenly, knowing he was right, but sure somehow that she was right as well. In these past few months, she'd been forced for the first time in her life to stand on her own, to make quick decisions. Sometimes, many times, she had made the wrong ones, but this time—

"You didn't rob me," she insisted, "and if you'd wanted to take advantage of my situation, you would have already done so."

"Maybe I wanted something else that night. Maybe I thought you had someone waiting for you at home. Or I was just waiting for you to recover from childbirth. Maybe I was just waiting for some guaranteed time alone."

"I don't think your friend Ada is the type who consorts with criminals. And if one of us is a stalker, it would be me." She raised her chin and stared him in the eye.

"As I said, you've thanked me. You can go now."

He was, no doubt, right. This wasn't Mayberry, a world where every stranger eventually became a friend and every problem was resolved in thirty minutes. Still, this was her world now, hers and Ruthie's. For the first time in her life she got to make the rules, to decide how she and her child would go on for the rest of their lives. She was on the run, frightened and uncertain of almost everything. Still, she chose not to run from this man, but to do what she had to if she were ever to be truly free.

She managed a weak smile. "You saved our lives, you spent a lot of money on us. Words couldn't possibly be enough."

"And if I say they are?"

"You don't get to decide. As I said, a mother needs to teach her child the right way to live."

"She's just a baby."

Ruthie had started to coo, and the man looked at her as if Molly had a monster wrapped in a blanket. And yet his words had been almost gentle, softer than anything he'd said thus far.

"Maybe so, but I'm not, and I can't let anyone pay my way," Molly argued. She shifted Ruthie in her arms and the blanket fell away. The man glanced at the baby, then quickly raised his eyes as though he couldn't bear to look at the child.

"I'm not trying to be a pest, but—look, I work in the bakery down the street. I can pay you a little at a time. You'll tell me the amount?"

She could see by the dark wariness of the stranger's eyes that she had gone too far and that he wasn't going to tell her a thing.

"All right then, I'll decide when I've paid enough. I'll do some research, ask some questions."

He reached out and just barely touched her arm. She gasped at the unexpected contact. "Don't ask questions. Don't come back," he said, and he let her go.

In only a moment, he had slipped away into the darkness. As if he'd never been there and never would be again.

Molly felt suddenly alone. His touch had been brief but warm, and no one touched her anymore. She didn't let them.

She looked down at the baby, who was starting to yawn.

"Well, pumpkin," Molly said with a long sigh and an attempt at a fake smile. "I think that went rather well, don't you?"

The baby blinked once, then blew a small bubble.

"Come on, Ruthie Ann," Molly said, cuddling her daughter close. "Let's go home and get some rest. This paying your debts business is pretty tough stuff. But don't you worry. This time I have a plan, and we're in control."

But a few minutes later when a stranger in a store

told her she looked familiar and that she had a beautiful baby, Molly felt panic surge through her. She had tried to find a place where she and Ruthie could be anonymous, where they could blend in and disappear.

So maybe she and her unnamed hero had something in common, after all. Neither of them wanted to attract attention. She knew her own reasons. She wondered what his were.

Chapter 3

"Who in the world do you think she is?" Cecily Thommins stared at Ada, part of a group of four women who had been gathering together to play cards, share celebrity gossip and stories of the neighborhood for forty years. Cecily was squinting behind her oversize glasses, staring through the basement window at the young woman sweeping the street in front of the apartment building.

"What do you mean, who do I think she is? She's Molly, that's all. That's all there is to know," Ada grumbled.

"Ha!" Fran, the one with the violet-tinted beehive said. "There's always more to know. You *wish* you knew more, but you don't. I know you, Ada. Your wheels are always turning. You're always wondering and spinning the possibilities. Anyway, if you don't know anything about her but her name, what, for land's sake, is she doing sweeping your front stoop?"

Ada shrugged. "I met her maybe six weeks ago, did her a little favor. She asked if she could do something in return, so I let her do a little basic cleanup, but I don't know anything. Still, you're right, Fran. I can't help but wonder where she came from. There's just something about her that makes me think…oh, I don't know…like I knew her once before."

Dora snorted, her artificial black helmet of hair scraping against the linebacker shoulders of her purple cardigan. "A pretty young thing like that? You didn't know her while I've been around, and I've been around you a long time. Besides, what would she know of moldy old ladies like us?"

Ada turned and gave her friend a hard stare. "You want to call yourself moldy? You do that, but leave me out. I'll let you know when I feel moldy, and anyway, I didn't say I'd met the girl before. I just said she made me feel like I had. She's…nice, you know? Or maybe you don't know. You probably wouldn't know nice if it bit you on the butt."

Dora returned the stare. "She's got you flummoxed, doesn't she? That's why you're acting so bitchy today."

Fran tutted and laid down a card. "I see what you mean, Ada. The girl has kind eyes."

Ada glanced out the window again. "No, she has

worried eyes. She's young and alone with a baby. What's that about?"

"Hey, who knows? It happens sometimes, but it's really not your problem, is it?" Dora asked.

"I didn't say it was, did I? There's just something about her."

"You said that already. Now will you shut up and play? If we're going to brunch and the matinee, we've got to finish this game soon."

Ada shut up. She wondered what Seth would say if he knew Molly had been here. He wouldn't be happy. Well, too bad. To hell with Seth. She adored him, but this was her building, and she liked Molly. She would invite her around if she felt like it. And sooner or later she would figure out what it was about Molly Delavan that was bugging her...

Seth woke up groggy and realized that he had only been asleep a few hours. The blurry red numbers on his clock said it all. Nine o'clock on a Sunday morning when most of Chicago traffic had yet to come to life and hit the potholes, so what was it that had awakened him? A noise of some sort. There it was. It sounded like...hell, it sounded like a woman. Not an older woman, either. She was humming. Right outside the building.

"Can't be." But he knew he was wrong. Seth sat up, instantly and fully awake. He could have looked out the window to confirm his suspicions, but the truth was that he didn't need to. Instead he threw his clothes on and stumbled down the stairs onto the entrance landing of the building. He glanced out the fanlight window next to the door in the vestibule.

The woman was as beautiful as he was scarred. Even with her long brown hair tied back, a jacket that had been almost worn to death and a tear in her jeans that revealed a slender patch of naked skin, she looked lovely.

She was wielding a broom, cleaning the walkway, and her lips were moving even though the humming had stopped. The reason became clear when he saw that she was talking to the baby strapped to her front.

His heart began to thunder as he drew close and got a better view, muttering a curse beneath his breath.

"A woman and a baby," he whispered. "Two things I could sure as hell do without." He ran his hand over the scars on his cheek, raised his brows to feel the tightening of the damaged skin on his forehead and felt a sense of gratitude for his protection. With a face like this one, women seldom wanted him anymore. Not in the bright light of day, anyway.

But this woman was obviously and woefully unaware of her own safety in this part of town where the occasional old holdout apartment building shared the street with grimy, tired stores fronted by burglar bars. She had a small pack belted around her slender hips. It flapped against her with every move she made, inviting a thief's attention. Wrapped up in what she was doing, she wouldn't even see what was happening around her. She still hadn't noticed that he was watching her.

Why *was* she here? Their conversation the day before had taken place half a block from here, not right on his doorstep, and yet…here she was.

Ada, he remembered. She'd been talking to Ada a lot.

Seth pushed back the heavy wooden door and stepped out.

"So, how far are we going to take this, lady?" he asked. "This lesson thing?"

She jumped, then collected herself. She looked up, smiling slightly, as though she welcomed his intrusion and his brusque manner, and he noticed a slight smudge of dirt on her cheek. Dark against the pink. Harsh against the softness. Begging for a man's hand to curve close and caress.

He forced himself to ignore that thought. At least he tried to. The tightness in his chest remained.

"Good morning," she said, "and my name's Molly. Molly Delavan, not lady."

"I know your first name. You told them at the hospital."

But he didn't want to call her by a name. He didn't want her to become real.

"And your name is…" she prompted.

He glared at her. "If you know where I live, you must know who I am."

She raised a delicate brow. "I know that your friend, Ada, lives here. And now you've shown up here, too."

So she hadn't been certain that he lived here. Seth deepened his frown, chastising himself for not being more careful. He was always careful. He stayed alive and working and sane by being careful.

"Seth McCabe," he finally said, giving in. Maybe she was one of those obstinate types who only pushed until they got their way. Then, satisfied, they trotted off to cause trouble somewhere else.

Leaning her broom against the crusty brick of the building, she held out her hand. "Thank you for that, Mr. McCabe."

Seth stared at her hand as though she'd just offered him a great white shark to cozy up to. Touching was something he didn't do much of. Not with this kind of woman, anyway.

But she was waiting and he was beginning to get the feeling that she would wait forever if he didn't take her hand. So he did. Slowly. Deliberately. Insultingly slow and suggestively, he slid his skin over hers, dragging his fingers against her palm, brushing the pads of her fingertips with his own, trying to warn her to back off. He claimed what she was offering as slick need suddenly sluiced through him. His body tightened, hardened, tensed. He fought it, stilling his hand and as much of his mind as he could manage.

Then, having shut down whatever senses he could, when he had almost mastered himself and she was off guard, he gave a quick tug, tumbling Molly toward him.

She gasped, but he didn't stop.

With one hand he curved his arm out to shelter her and the child. With the other, he unzipped her hip pack with a deft, quick touch and removed her wallet, holding it out to her.

Her sharp, rapid breathing, the way she automatically cuddled her baby close, made him feel sick. With rage at himself. With anger at her for being here and making him aware of her and how vulnerable she was. This wasn't right. He didn't do this stuff. He hated the thought that he had frightened her, but…

"Don't be so trusting, lady. Molly," he said, correcting himself. "You can't just choose a stranger and follow him around without taking a risk."

She sucked in her lip. "I know that, but…you didn't hurt me," she said obstinately, accepting the wallet and putting it back where it belonged, her breathing a bit too rushed. Maybe he hadn't physically harmed her, but he had scared her some. Perhaps she would be more aware from now on. Or she might run away and never come back. That would work, too.

"I *could* have hurt you," he pointed out, his voice rough edged and unrelenting. "I could have overpowered you easily, and anyone else could have, too. You have to be alert and ready for anything when you're on the street."

She nodded. "I know that. I read things. I realize that the city has its dark side. But right now it's a beautiful Sunday morning. The sun is shining."

Yes, he was aware of that. Well aware, because he rarely saw the morning sun. Usually, he slept in after being out much of the night, but he hadn't been sleeping well lately. The reason couldn't be important.

Since his frowns hadn't worked on her, he tried staring directly into her eyes. "Bad things happen in sunlight as well as darkness, Ms. Delavan."

"Yes, I know that, too." This time it was as if he had finally punctured her happiness. There was a sudden solemnity to her that hadn't been there before. The woman knew what he was talking about. "But I still have every right to be here."

He couldn't help himself then. The slightest of smiles tugged at his lips.

"Has anyone ever told you no, Ms. Delavan?"

She bit her lip, her color rising. "Plenty of times."

"Have you ever actually listened?"

"Usually, but this is different."

He didn't want to ask why it was different. "I have to tell you that you are a total pain in the—" he looked down at the baby she held so close "—the rear."

"And you are keeping me from my task, Mr. McCabe," Molly said, indicating the broom she had set aside. "Ada loaned out her car that night. I owe her, too, so I've talked her into letting me do a little cleanup work for the next week."

A week? She was going to be underfoot for an entire week? The dismay he was feeling must have shown through.

"It's for Ada," she insisted. "Although, since she owns the building, you might have to put up with me."

He took a deep breath. "It would be best if we didn't cross paths too much."

Those brown eyes looked suddenly wounded, but she quickly masked her reaction. "I keep strange hours," he said, wondering why he was explaining. "I wouldn't want to happen upon you and scare you."

"I'm not afraid of you. You gave my wallet back."

But that wasn't what he meant. He didn't even mean the face, since she'd obviously chosen to look past it in her determination to be a good citizen. What he meant was that the woman made heat snake through him every time she opened her mouth, every time she moved the slightest bit. He was aware of every inch of luscious skin she owned, the parts he could see and those that he could only imagine. And, as a writer, he had a vivid imagination.

It didn't bear thinking of. He couldn't get close to people. Not anymore. The fact that he wanted to touch this innocent, trusting woman, to feel his fingers skimming more than her palm, unnerved him. He hadn't desired anything in a long time, and desire was a dangerous business, one he didn't engage in except on the most rudimentary level.

He must have gone too long without seeing to his needs. He'd have to do something about that, help himself manage to stay human a bit longer.

When he still hadn't spoken, she sighed. "I'll come after work, midafternoon. Ada will let me in," she said quietly.

Seth turned so swiftly that the words had barely left her mouth before his hand had clamped down on her wrist.

"Let you in? What for?"

She took long, deep breaths. She stared down at where his fingers curled against her pale skin. He had loosened his grasp, but he still held her, still felt the contact, the burning, the ache just touching her was causing him.

"I promised Ada I'd clean her building top to bottom. She's not a young woman, Seth."

"And I'm capable of cleaning up after myself," he advised. He raised one finger, then another, and another, slowly releasing her. "Don't come near my place."

"I'm—I'm sorry," she said on a whisper. "Cleaning is part of what I do at the bakery every day. It's how I support Ruthie and myself. I'll be gone once I've paid my debts. I don't like nosy people, either, and I never intended to spy or intrude."

"I didn't accuse you of that," he said, but he didn't back away from his restrictions. Letting someone in risked familiarity, breaking down walls he meant to build higher.

"Never mind," she said. "You want privacy? I'll confine myself to Ada's apartment and the shared areas of the building. You won't even know I'm here, except on payday. I think I can afford ten or twenty dollars a week."

He doubted that very much, judging by the way she was dressed, but he'd already learned that it was pointless to argue about the matter of what she saw as her "debt."

"Ten will do," he tried. She reached for her broom again.

He took it from her hand. "It's Sunday. Go home and play with your kid," he told her. "Ada won't mind. And, Molly?"

She looked up at him as he pulled back the door and placed his foot on the step leading inside.

"Yes, Seth?"

"Thank you for helping Ada, even if I still say this is completely unnecessary and frivolous."

This time *her* hand clamped down on his arm. "Seth?"

He cocked his head, waiting.

"I'm never frivolous. Don't patronize me. Everything I do, I do for a reason."

"Good. Keep it that way. It'll keep you safe."

And it was clear that safety was an issue, he thought as he moved back into his apartment. The question was, where did the greatest danger lie? On the street, or here locked up behind these four walls she'd wanted to breach?

He didn't know and didn't care to look that deeply into his psyche anymore, and so he flicked on his computer, turned the volume up on his stereo and tried to write his demons away as Rachmaninoff filled his apartment, swelling into the shadowy empty spaces. He punched at the keys, sidestepping his visions of dark brown eyes peeking through a curtain of light brown hair. And he waited for the night, when the struggles of the street meant keeping his wits about him or risking death at the hands of a stranger. No daydreaming allowed.

Which was just too bad because as he stepped out the door into a black cloudless night that favored those bent on evil, his first thought was that he hoped Molly and her baby were safe behind locked doors.

And then he plunged into the darkness.

Seth thought he had put the topic of women in jeopardy out of his mind completely until early the next evening when he rose and retrieved his mail. Returning to his apartment, he absentmindedly fingered the new knife nick of the night before, barely an inch shy of his jugular.

But that didn't matter. What mattered was that he was holding a long, slender envelope addressed in deep black familiar slashes. His own writing.

Seth frowned at the rounded "Return to Sender" scrawled in violet across the front.

"Damn it to hell," he said, tearing the envelope in half. The contents, twin ragged pieces of a check fell out. His sister had returned his offering just as she'd returned the last...and the one before that. He'd hoped that with time she would allow at least this much, but no. She didn't want his help.

He couldn't blame her. His help had only hurt her in the past. He'd destroyed her hopes, her future.

If he were wise, he'd leave her alone completely— or more completely than he already did.

Seth was still thinking that when he heard familiar humming outside his door. The soft, low notes drifted to him, a vision of Molly's brown eyes and softly parted lips nagged at him, and heat slithered down through his body, pooling in his groin.

Pavlovian. Ignore it, he ordered himself.

He forced in a long, slow breath, then moved back into the bowels of the apartment. Not that it mattered. He could still feel her presence; he could imagine the innocent smile she would be wearing. She'd be glancing down at her baby now and then. And no matter what she claimed about her street sense, the distraction of her child would put her in danger.

Seth closed his eyes. He knew far too much about the danger that breathed strong and silently in the world. He'd felt it, smelled it, wallowed in it. It came alive at night.

At the sound of the downstairs door clicking shut, he almost moved to the window and looked out, stopping just in time. Next thing you knew, he'd be following her outside, offering to walk her home, as if he were any other man.

But he wasn't, hadn't been for years and never would be. Still, he couldn't help noticing how dark it suddenly seemed. Night had fallen like a swift sledgehammer, and Molly was still out.

Damn it. He didn't want to think about that. Not a bit, but his feet carried him to the window. Molly had stopped a block away, trapped in the purple-white glare of a streetlight.

What in hell was going on? And what was that stranger doing approaching her? Surely she wasn't smiling and reaching into her fanny pack to dig out some change.

Seth let out a roar. Slamming out the door past his newly sparkling hallway, he thundered down the stairs. He threw the glass door back and turned in the direction Molly had gone.

She wasn't going to like this. Neither was he, but someone had darn well better make sure that if the woman was going to live in a place like this, she knew something about survival. If someone didn't teach her, something bad was going to happen sooner or later, and then there would be hell to pay.

With a growl low in the back of his throat, Seth took off after the damned infuriating woman.

"A woman like Molly doesn't just disappear into the ether," the dark-haired man in the police uniform said to another man dressed in a nondescript outfit of gray sweats and a gray cap. "People notice those cover-girl looks. Tough to hide."

"Yeah, well I haven't found her yet, and you haven't given me much incentive to dig deeper."

One thick blue-clad arm shot out and grasped the shorter man by the shirtfront, chest hair caught up in the fabric. "You'll get your money, Dom, when I get what I want. You'll get more if you get her to me fast."

The man in gray twisted, trying to get away, but the cop dragged him closer, getting in his face.

"What about the baby?" Dom wrenched out the words as his captor squeezed tighter, separating skin from hair. "What if she's ditched the baby? Women do, you know."

"Not her, so don't try to tell me she has. Besides, it's a package deal. I want them both. I'll get them both. Find them. People like Molly don't just disappear. She's around. You get her and bring her to me. Do whatever it takes other than messing up her looks or the kid's. Anything it takes as long as it doesn't show. Then I'll take over. You'll get your money, and I'll get what I've been waiting for all my life."

"Money?"

"A gold mine. Molly's worth something, but the kid...the kid's going to make me one really rich bastard, and nothing is going to stop that from happening."

Chapter 4

Molly had barely made it back into her apartment when the door began to shake with a thunderous pounding.

Gasping, she clutched Ruthie and jumped back a step.

The pounding began again, and she quietly scooted near enough to look out the peephole. Seth stood there glaring, ready to knock again when she pulled open the door.

"What the hell do you think you're doing?" he demanded.

She blinked and clutched Ruthie closer. "I don't think I'm the one who needs to answer that question." She stared pointedly at his fist, which was still raised.

He lowered his hand, but he didn't look the slightest bit apologetic. "I saw you give money to that guy on the street."

"He needed money."

A low muffled groan escaped Seth. "He can get it from someone else."

She gave him a long stare, then turned her back on him and moved into the next room toward a small crib placed next to the bed. Gently she lowered Ruthie into it, then returned to face Seth, who was still standing in the doorway.

"Come inside," she said.

He frowned. "No."

"I won't bite."

Looking to the side, he shook his head. "You just don't get it, do you? This is Chicago. You know, big city."

"The City of Big Shoulders," she supplied.

"No, a city, as in crime statistics. This part of town is worse than most."

"I know that," she finally said softly. "But—" She didn't want to let him know that it was all she could afford right now.

He made a slashing motion with his hand, cutting her off. "I'm not judging you," he said.

"You are."

"All right, I am, but…"

"Let me guess. It's for my own good."

"Exactly."

She sighed. "I think I know that, and, don't get me wrong, I'm incredibly grateful, but I have a child now. I don't want her to grow up afraid of everything, even if—"

"Go on."

"Even if there are some very real things to be afraid of. That man I gave the money to had kind eyes. He didn't try to get close to me. He didn't follow me. I watched."

"*I* followed you."

"Yes, and you're right if you mean that I didn't know you were there, but I did watch the other man. He turned off the street two blocks from your place."

"Could have been a ploy to make you feel safe."

She shivered, knowing he was right.

"I have to have some good in my life," she said suddenly, her voice filled with more anguish than she wanted to reveal. "I need some sense of decency."

His eyes, which had been so hard, suddenly softened. "All right then, I won't lecture anymore. I won't bark."

"Or pound," she said.

A hint of a smile almost lifted his lips. "Or pound," he agreed. "At least not today. But someone definitely needs to teach you something about living in a city this size. I'll bet you grew up in the country."

Suddenly her breathing came hard, fast. She felt as if she was suffocating. Questions about her origins could do that now. She struggled for an answer that would appease him.

"Forget that," he said abruptly. "I don't want to know. Not anything. Just be smart. I don't have time to baby-sit you and the kid. Do yourself a favor. Ask some questions of someone who knows how to go on. Educate yourself. Get some street smarts. Maybe from those people you work for."

"Mr. Alex, the baker? The man who feeds the pigeons at first light and who passes out cups of coffee to anyone who begs outside his door, as long as they're gone by the time the sun rises and the store opens? The man who's been robbed three times in the past ten years?"

Seth blinked. "I hear he's a good man, and he's probably learned a few things, but no, he's probably not cynical enough for what I have in mind." His voice grated low, and Molly almost forgot what they were talking about for a minute, even though she knew that he was right. She hated being afraid, and so she'd been rebellious, telling herself that she wouldn't let Kevin Rickman scare her. But the truth was that he *did* scare her. He terrified her, and she needed to know how to be more evasive, maybe not to avoid the panhandlers but to avoid the real danger that could show up at any time.

Slowly she nodded and looked up at Seth. He was studying her carefully, those gray eyes fierce and probing, as if he could see everything there was to see about her. Her secrets, her longings. Molly bit her lip. "If Mr. Alex won't do, what do you have in mind?" she asked.

He shrugged and began to back farther into the hallway. "You're helping Ada. She's a good one to talk to. Ada knows the ropes. No one puts anything past her."

Ada, that sweetly cranky old woman. A woman who might ask questions, but—he was right. Ada might give answers, as well.

"You talk to her," he said. "I'll tell her what you need to know."

"Why don't *you* just tell me?" she asked, and he stopped in midstride, as if she'd touched him in a game of freeze tag. His face was a mask, but she could tell he wasn't happy.

"Ask Ada to help you," he told her. "Don't forget. You have to stay safe for—" he nodded toward the crib "—her."

The truth crashed into Molly. Seth was right. "I will."

"Don't forget."

"I won't." But she couldn't help adding, "I still don't think that man would have hurt me. He wasn't the type."

"Maybe not. Probably not. But now that he knows you're a soft touch, he'll probably approach you again. That'll bring others your way."

"How would he remember me?" She tried to hide her panic.

Seth's gaze held hers, and she couldn't look away. "He'll remember," he said, and she almost stopped breathing.

She barely managed to nod.

"I'll be more careful. I'll talk to Ada." But fear clutched at her. Would the panhandler remember her?

Maybe. Probably not that many people stopped to place money in his palm in spite of his kind eyes.

But it was not the panhandler's eyes she was remembering long after Seth had gone. And when she looked out the window five minutes later, she almost thought she saw a movement in the shadows, a trace of a tattered army jacket and the dark glint of gray eyes in the small bit of light available.

Looking again, she saw that she was wrong. There was no one there.

She should have been elated, relieved. So why did she suddenly feel so empty and so terribly alone?

The bakery had been busy today, and Molly's back was aching when she showed up at Ada's, knocked on the door and went to get a broom.

"Floor doesn't need sweeping today," Ada said, studying her, a suspicious look in her eyes. "And you don't need to keep that baby strapped to you when you're working. Bet this one doesn't cry much."

The hopeful sound in Ada's voice broke through Molly's fatigue, and she couldn't help smiling. "No, she's very good."

Ada stared at Ruthie, who was cooing quietly. "She's gonna be a charmer."

The old woman's voice was wistful and Molly wondered if Ada had ever married and had children. She didn't like to pry, though, especially given her own circumstances.

"Would you like to hold her?" she asked, following Ada's earlier cue.

A strange look came over Ada, the wrinkles in her face increasing, and Molly realized that the woman was smiling. Ada held out her arms.

When Molly placed Ruthie into them, the baby let out a small sound that could only be interpreted as baby delight. "She likes you."

"'Course she does," Ada said. "Now you sit down there, and let's have a chat. Seth told me that you were going to ask me to tell you a few things about staying alive and in full control of your pocketbook when the dogs are snapping at your heels."

Molly chuckled. "Well, I hadn't thought of it that way."

"See?" Ada said, shaking her head. "That's your first mistake. You've got to be aware. You've got to be suspicious of everyone and everything."

"Even you?"

Ada gave her a disbelieving stare. "Heck, yes. It's the ones that look weak and old that catch you off guard. You think you're going to hurt them, and the next thing you know, they've snatched the watch right off your wrist and you don't even realize it until hours later."

Molly crossed her arms over her chest. "I don't believe you would hurt me."

Ada clutched her chest. "Bless my black heart, he was right. You're as innocent as a baby robin."

Molly didn't bother asking what else Seth had said

about her. She wrinkled her nose and reached for the broom she had put down. "You lent me your blanket so I wouldn't freeze when you had never seen me in your life. Seth drove me to the hospital." She didn't reveal that he had paid her way. That was too personal and she was pretty sure that he didn't want anyone, including herself, to know that. "I refuse to think that that was the work of two untrustworthy types."

"No, it was instinct. I was half-asleep and Seth was most likely shocked to find you half-dead on the sidewalk. You don't know a thing about us."

"So tell me."

Ada pursed her lips. "Everybody has secrets. I don't ask and I don't tell. Yours or anyone else's, either."

"All right," Molly said with a sigh. "At least tell me about this neighborhood. That much I need to know."

"Guess that wouldn't hurt." Ada rocked Ruthie, who grunted her satisfaction. "It's a changing neighborhood, but then it's always seemed like it's changing. Lately it's changed for the worse. People who are down on their luck, newcomers who haven't found their way yet. Others who don't want to find their way and would rather prey on the ones who are just trying to make a living. Lots of people living on the streets, lots of people begging, not all of them for good reasons, either."

She scowled at Molly and Molly figured that Seth had mentioned the panhandler. She opened her mouth to tell Ada what she had told Seth, but Ada shook her head. "Don't bother. I can tell you've got a soft heart, but you can't afford to be soft. You've got a baby."

Molly hesitated, then she nodded curtly. "I know. You're right. So I don't give handouts."

"And you make sure that when you walk, you keep well away from the buildings. That way no one can grab you from some hiding place and rob you. You wear your purse under your coat, even if it looks funny. You never daydream on the street. You stare people in the eyes. Makes them nervous." She stared at Molly. Obviously, Ada considered herself an expert at making people nervous, even though Molly considered her expression sweetly endearing. Still, she knew better than to say so.

"You get yourself a can of that pepper spray, an alarm, a flashlight and at least one sharp object which you stash somewhere where you can get to it easily. You use your lungs if you have to, and any other body parts you need if things go wrong. Never be afraid to kick. If you're wrong, you can apologize and say that you thought the man was your ex-husband."

Ada grumbled at that, and once again Molly wondered what Ada's life had once been like. Maybe they weren't so very different after all.

"Anything else?"

"Yes."

Ada took a deep breath and Molly waited.

"You do anything and everything you have to in order to keep yourself and this baby safe and don't worry about the consequences."

Molly nodded. "Thank you. I will, Ada. I promise." She rose slowly and started to get back to work. "Would you—will you watch Ruthie while I finish up? She seems to like you."

Ada let out something that sounded like a cough but was probably a chuckle. "She's a little honey, and of course I'll watch her, but I'm not done yet."

There was something in her voice...

Molly tensed. "Yes?"

"Don't go falling for him. He'll hurt you real bad."

"Excuse me?" Molly's breath hitched in her throat.

Ada stuck her thumb up in the air, motioning toward the top floor where Seth lived. "Seth. He's a good man, but he's not for you. He's not for any woman. He's got issues. I don't know what they are, but he's got 'em by the bushel."

That was no secret to Molly, and it was probably a good thing. She had issues, too.

"I'm not looking for a man. On any level," she said.

"Humph." Ada looked at Ruthie with disbelief. "I think your mama is stretching the truth. Most women want a man for one or two things."

"Not me." Molly stood her ground, refusing to say more.

And then Ada smiled. Molly wasn't sure what it meant, and she wasn't sure it was a good thing.

"I'm not interested in Seth," she insisted, but she wasn't sure if she was saying the words for Ada's sake or her own.

Ada stared at her. "You have an interesting voice," she said, and then she didn't say anything more.

And Molly breathed a little faster. She had always been told that her voice was a little different, and it was one thing about herself that she hadn't been able to change. She wanted to say something flippant, but she couldn't think of a thing.

"I'll just sweep a little," was all she could come up with, and Ada nodded.

"Ruthie and I will read the paper together. I like that 'Mean Streets' column."

"'Mean Streets'?"

Ada shrugged. "It's about what happens in the city at night in the part of town most people don't want to go near. This writer, Nick Dawson, he really makes those people come alive. He tells their stories. Makes you want to do something to help, to bring them into the light."

Molly swallowed hard as she glanced at the column Ada was pointing to. She wouldn't want her story to be told. Not that it would. This neighborhood might be down on its luck, but after reading three paragraphs, she could see that this wasn't bad enough to be the type of place Nick Dawson wrote about, and she wasn't the kind of subject he was interested in.

Anyway, he wouldn't find out about her.

Something was different tonight. Seth was on the hunt. There was a rage brewing inside him, one he didn't want to give in to but that wouldn't let him go nonetheless.

He knew why. Ada had spoken to him about her talk with Molly, but he was still worried. He couldn't shake the thought that Molly didn't have a clue about how dangerous the streets were. She was an innocent waiting to be wounded.

Like his sister had been. Shannon had only been fourteen when their parents had perished and so she had been left to the care of an ignorant boy barely out of high school himself. He'd tried so hard to protect her. Too hard, since his strict overprotective efforts had only driven her to run away to live on the streets. So yes, he knew the dangers of mishandling this situation with Molly. Because of his poor judgment, Shannon's life had been irreparably damaged.

Damn him to hell if he repeated the mistakes of the past. He didn't want to be a protector, but he had to be sure Molly at least knew some basic safety skills. And he knew why he cared.

"Guilt from the past." No matter. It had to be done. Then he could sleep, or as well as a man like him ever slept.

He gazed around him at the awakening world of those who lived on the streets, a place that came alive for a time at night when everyone else went inside.

There was Rip, a man who picked old clothes out of garbage bins and tore holes in them in places, so that no one else would be tempted to steal them. No real names here, at least not on this stretch of the city. Everyone seemed to have something to hide. Which was fine.

He wasn't here to reveal their secrets, but to make sure that no one forgot they existed. His sister had been mistreated while on the streets. So, he worked to make sure the world knew that these people still counted no matter how dirty and strange they might seem to so-called normal citizens.

The rumor was that Rip used to be an investment banker. Might be the truth. Might be a whopper of a lie. Didn't matter. What mattered was that somewhere beneath the grime and ripped clothing and compulsive behavior, he was still human, still a man. As were Coats and Don't Look and Snap, names that had been earned on the street and that told nothing of who these men and women had once been in former lives. They were also names that didn't get mentioned too often, because no one talked very much around here.

Which was a good thing, Seth supposed. What a man didn't say was sometimes much more important than what he did say. And what he did say had better be thought through carefully. He was always careful about what he wrote concerning those who drifted through life and death on the streets.

He was always careful about everything, only allowing himself to write about each part of town he covered for a short while before moving on to another. So what was that reckless business of following Molly about? Why did she keep creeping into his consciousness when he least expected it?

"Don't go there," he warned himself.

"Don't go where, Lightning?" Shuffle asked, referring to the speed with which Seth had once thrown a man who had attacked him.

"Does it matter?" Seth asked. "Plenty of places a man should steer clear of."

"Like in front of your fists?" the man asked, laughing out loud.

Seth dredged up an edgy smile. "You don't have to worry, Shuffle. I don't use my fists unless I have to."

And I only get involved with a woman if I have to, he thought. Right now he had to help Molly, and then he had to step away, because if he didn't...if he didn't...

A vision of Molly's brown eyes and soft lips slid into his consciousness. Her lips looked...incredibly appetizing.

Seth took a deep breath and shook away the thought. "Let's go settle down for the night," he told Shuffle.

And for most of the night he kept any errant thoughts at bay. He had to stay alert to stay alive. His senses were still on autopilot when he trudged away and toward home just before dawn.

Not far from home, he sensed movement from out of the corner of his eye. Someone trailing him. Turning quickly, he saw a shadow, a man's arm disappearing around a corner.

Instantly, Seth was the hunter, the wolf whose senses never sleep. His nostrils flared as if to scent his prey, and he slipped around the corner to find...nothing.

For a minute, anger flayed him, regret that he had let a potential mugger escape.

But the man was gone and there was one good thing about the situation. He had not been heading in Molly's direction.

He would tell Ada to be extra careful from here on out, and he would keep an eye open, but chances were good, now that he had been seen, that the man would not come back. It was the way of the amateur criminal. He ran away, found another target. There was always another target.

"Okay, but not me or mine," Seth said, and when he thought *mine* he did his best not to think of a pretty brown-haired woman.

But he failed. And so he slammed the door a little too hard when he came inside. His steps on the graying cabbage-rose carpet on the stairs were heavier than usual.

"Bad night?" Ada asked, leaning her head out the door, her gray hair wrapped around purple foam curlers.

He gave her a look, one that said, *Don't push it, Ada.*

She cackled. "Been thinkin' about her, haven't you?"

"Who?"

But she only laughed harder.

Chapter 5

Jeff Payton was breathing hard as he sprinted toward his own part of town and the closest taxicab. He had nearly been caught back there, had actually heard the man's breathing as he swooped around the corner. If not for a conveniently open Dumpster, he would have been caught, possibly beaten.

How did Nick Dawson *do* this stuff? Dawson, Jeff's personal hero and the writer of the "Mean Streets" column, tailed homeless men like the one Jeff had been following, a man who appeared to be the leader of the men Jeff had watched last night. A writer like Nick had to know how to blend in. What kind of a background would he have?

Whatever he was, somehow the man earned the trust

of people who normally didn't trust anyone. He shadowed them and yet no one really knew who *he* was. Had anyone ever actually done a story on Nick Dawson himself? Had anyone ever even seen a picture?

"They will soon," Jeff whispered. "I'm the man who's going to nab this story."

Nick Dawson had to be brilliant. The world needed more men like him, and they needed to know more about him. So what if he wrote for Jeff's rival newspaper? That only made his boss more eager for him to figure out the puzzle. If he could do that…

"If I could do that, I could write features instead of obits," Jeff whispered. He could live his dream.

So yeah, risking his neck in this part of town was worth it. He just wished he knew what Nick Dawson looked like. That would make his search so much easier.

Work today had been long and hard, Molly thought two days after her talk with Ada, and she still had to do some work at Ada's, but the closer she got, the lighter her steps seemed.

"It's because I know Kevin is a morning person," Molly whispered to Ruthie, refusing to use the word *father* to describe the man who was threatening her daughter. "He won't be out looking for us after dark." Which it would be, soon. Of course her expectant attitude had nothing whatsoever to do with the top floor inhabitant of Ada's building.

"Seth won't even be out, anyway," she told her baby. "He works at night, so our paths won't cross."

But as she pushed open the outside door and entered the first floor, using the key Ada had given her, Molly breathed in deeply. Somewhere, mixed in with the scents of Ada's roast beef, aging plaster and the dying carnations Mr. Alex had let her take home with her yesterday and which she had placed in the hallway, there was a hint of man, of Seth.

Molly closed her eyes and then, realizing what she was doing, she halted her thoughts and knocked on Ada's door.

"It's Molly," she called out. "I'm just going to polish the woodwork on the first-floor landing today." She took Ruthie from her back carrier and lovingly deposited her in the portable playpen that had mysteriously appeared in the hall yesterday. The blankets and rubber toys inside all looked brand-new. She had mentioned this to Ada, who refused to say anything about the issue. So had it been Ada or Seth? She would never know.

At that moment Ada's door creaked open and Ada gave Molly one of her half-frown-half-smile looks. Her eyes darted to the baby kicking her toes in the playpen.

"Be careful not to stir up too much dust," she said. "Not good for a baby. But it's nice of you to do it. Some of my lady friends are coming over tomorrow, and besides, the upstairs hall hasn't been dusted in years." Her gaze shifted off Molly. "Too hard to climb up there, you know," she said, putting a hand on her back.

Molly frowned, suddenly concerned. "Ada, you should have said. I didn't think you wanted me up there, or I would have done it sooner."

Ada shook her head. "See there, you're doin' it again. Jumping in right now when you should have been wondering why I'm complaining about my back now when I've never complained about it before. Seth won't like that one bit."

Molly tried to ignore that comment. She didn't want to talk about Seth because she was afraid she would look too interested. "So…was this a trick suggestion? Has the upstairs really not been dusted?"

Ada's glance shifted away. "Might have been," she said. "Might not, too. I'm old. I forget things."

Molly was pretty sure that Ada didn't forget a thing, but she knew that the woman did have a soft spot for Seth. She wouldn't want him to be living in substandard conditions if she could help it. And she *was* old. Her mind was strong and clear, but going up and down stairs couldn't be good for her.

"I'll just check on how things look," Molly said, heading up the stairs.

"He'll raise hell if you go up there," Ada warned just as if she hadn't been the person to suggest Molly go work up there in the first place.

"I'm not afraid of hell," Molly said. But she *was* afraid of many things, including Kevin and including her reaction to Seth every time she got too near.

So why are you going up there? she asked herself.

Because the man probably doesn't take care of himself. If Ada doesn't go up there, who does?

Nobody, because he would never let anybody get close.

"I'm not going to bother Seth," she told herself and Ada. "I'm just going to make things a little nicer. I owe the man."

"All right, but make sure he knows it's you."

"Why?"

"Because I'm usually in bed by now, and if it's not me…"

Ada's voice echoed up the stairs, muffled by distance, and Molly stepped onto the landing. She registered the last of Ada's words just as the door in front of her flew open and Seth reached out and grabbed her by the arm.

She gave a sharp gasp.

"I told you," she thought she heard Ada say. "You two work it out. I'll look after this baby."

And then Molly heard Ada's door clicking shut. She looked up and stared straight into Seth's angry gray eyes.

"You would be up here…for what reason?" Seth asked, staring down into Molly's startled eyes. Her mouth was a pink *O* of surprise. She swallowed and licked her lips, and he became instantly aware that he was touching her, that he held her so near the tips of her breasts were nearly brushing his chest. He could feel the pulse of her blood beneath the soft skin his fingers held. The sudden urge to slide those fingers and touch even more of her was intense.

Instantly he released her and she cradled her arm like a child who has been bitten by a puppy she was petting. His first instinct was to reach out and examine the spot where he had been holding her, make sure he hadn't hurt her, but that would put him right back into undeniably dangerous territory.

"Molly? he asked again, more patiently, trying to forget about her silky flesh. "Why are you up here?"

She swallowed. "I came to dust."

"I told you to stay away."

Now she raised her chin. He almost smiled when she made the move from surprise to indignation. "It's Ada's building. She can't climb these stairs all the time just so you can have a clean hallway."

Seth raised one brow. "I can live with dust." He hoped the point he was trying to make was coming through loud and clear. *I can live with dust. I just can't live with you coming up here and being near me in this isolated space.*

"I wasn't intruding," she insisted.

"I didn't say you were."

And then she did it. She laughed.

"What?" he demanded.

"You very well *did* imply that I was intruding and you know it. Tell me, does that act work on everyone you meet?"

Seth frowned. He crossed his arms, legs braced wide. "What act?"

"That one." She touched his crossed arms, and that single light stroke of her fingertip made him catch his breath. "That I'm-a-big-bad-male-and-you'd-better-stay-away act."

Obviously it wasn't working on her, at least not in the way he'd intended. Couldn't she see what she was doing to him? Didn't she know how any male would react to being alone with her like this?

He didn't even bother answering her question. Instead, he simply studied her, watching her the way he had learned to watch others—for his work—and yet, this wasn't anything at all like work. He couldn't seem to look away.

Then he noticed it, the tiny tremor in her hand, the one she tried to still by flattening her palm against her stomach. He *was* scaring her. Her laugh, her bravado was all bluff. She was afraid of him.

Seth took a step back. "My apologies," he said, giving her a brief, tight nod to accentuate his point. "You're right, Molly. This is Ada's building. If she and you have an arrangement, then being here is your right."

He stepped back to retreat into his apartment, the door opening wider.

Molly took a deep breath. "Thank you," she said. "I need to do this. I know you don't want it." To her credit, despite her discomfort, she looked him full in the face, and so he could do no less than return the gesture. He gazed at her, even managed a small smile.

"I promise not to bite if you promise to be quick."

The smile she gave him in return was so warm and lovely that it almost hurt to look at her. Still, he looked. He also thought of something.

"Molly?"

She looked up, waiting.

"You're not doing this for anyone else, are you? That is, there aren't a whole group of people you're following around offering your services to?"

"Of course not!"

"Good."

"But if I owed someone else a favor, I would repay it in any way I could."

He couldn't keep back the growl that rumbled through him. "Don't accept any more favors, at least not from men who live around here. It's not safe. If you need help, you come to me or Ada."

"If I accept more help from you, I'll owe you more. I might have to actually step over your threshold and clean your apartment."

She said the words teasingly, and just for a second, he thought she glanced behind him into his living room. He knew what she would see, a place bare of adornment except for the two pictures hanging on the wall: an old family photo and one of his sister, the last one he'd taken. Instinctively he shifted his weight, blocking her view.

Molly stepped back, looking to one side. "But I wouldn't even suggest that unless I felt I had to," she added.

"You won't have to," he promised.

He closed the door so she could go on with her work. And so that he could retreat from all the inappropriate thoughts that her presence always seemed to stir up in him.

For ten seconds he cursed the day he had discovered Molly lying on his sidewalk. And then he retracted that thought. Because if he hadn't found her, someone else might have.

At least she was safe with him. Wasn't she?

It wasn't a big hallway. In fact, it wasn't much more than a small landing. There was a tiny table bearing a plastic flower arrangement that looked as if it had arrived several decades earlier, as well as a rather lumpy chair that appeared never to have been used, judging by the cloud of dust that rose when Molly just touched it.

Given the size of this space, she should have been able to clean it in minutes and make her escape. No big deal.

Except Seth was on the other side. Seth had touched her.

"In warning, you dolt," she reminded herself. Nevertheless her body had reacted as if he had been trying to coax her closer. Even now, the memory of his strong warm fingers made her heart clench, her breath flow in and out in short, shallow gulps. She touched her wrist, then pulled her fingers away.

How silly. How stupid.

"Just clean," she told herself. "And don't wonder about the picture of the pretty woman on his wall."

Good advice. She had no business even thinking about a man at this time. It was a man who was a threat to everything she held dear.

And hadn't Seth warned her that he, too, would be a danger to her?

So why couldn't she stop thinking about those haunted, angry gray eyes and those strong fingers? Why wasn't she listening to the very good advice he was giving her?

But she knew why. He had wrapped his fingers around her, but he hadn't hurt her at all.

At least not yet.

"Up here again, Ada?"

"Just came to see what she did to your landing," Ada said as Seth lounged in his doorway.

"She came back and put flowers on the table. She dusted every nook and cranny. You should be happy, since you're always intimating that I live like a slob."

"You do live like a slob," Ada said pointedly. "You don't like her being around here, do you?"

Seth shifted his weight. "I don't like her being in this neighborhood at all. She's young and pretty and she attracts the wrong kind of person."

"You?"

Seth blinked, but he refused to rise to the bait. "You know I'm immune."

Ada cackled. "I don't know anything of the kind. I know you'd like to be immune, but I haven't noticed you tossing her down the stairs, and heaven knows, I've seen you chase away scores of others from our doorstep, both male and female."

"I don't chase them. I look at them."

"And they run. She doesn't."

He rubbed his jaw. "She should."

"Maybe she knows you better than the others."

"She doesn't know anything about me, and neither do you."

Ada shrugged. "True, but I know all I want to. Maybe she does, too. What I want to know is where I've seen her before." She frowned.

Instantly Seth was alert and at attention. "What do you mean?"

"I mean she looks awfully familiar. Don't you see it?"

He searched his memory and called up a picture of Molly with her upturned lips and doelike brown eyes. He didn't like thinking of her, because thinking made him want to touch.

"I never saw her before that day her baby was born." And she wasn't the type any man forgot.

"Hmm, you're pretty observant with those brooding eyes of yours. I thought you might remember something, because I just know there's something about her. I know her, somehow."

"Maybe you just want to. She and her baby have become your pet project."

Ada gave him one of those don't-think-you-fool-me looks she was so good at. "I suppose you're not interested."

"Suppose all you want, Ada. Just don't think that anything good can come of her being around here all the time."

"Hah! I gave up matchmaking years ago. Besides, I wouldn't match Molly with a man like you. You'd only end up breaking her heart."

"Damn straight."

"Or your own," she added. "And I like you too much to see you broken that way."

Seth blinked. He was about to open his mouth to protest that there was no possibility of Molly hurting him in any way when Ada held up her hand.

"I've seen your sister on the street twice in the past week."

"Here?"

She shook her head. "Around. She looks unhappy. Maybe you could…"

"No. I'm the one who made her unhappy. And I'm not going to hurt her anymore."

"You seem to spend a lot of time worrying about women you refuse to have anything to do with, Seth. I'd watch that if I were you. Could be harmful to your peace of mind."

He laughed. "What's peace of mind, Ada?"

"It's what you feel when Molly smiles, Seth," she said with a smile of her own, and she turned to head back down the stairs.

But she was wrong, he thought. Peace of mind wasn't what he felt when Molly smiled. He felt... heated, lustful, frustrated.

And there wasn't a damn thing he could do about any of that, was there?

Nothing but hit the streets and work, he thought, noting that tonight was darker than usual. The moon was waning.

It was just the kind of night he liked the most. In such total darkness, the streets came alive.

And so could he, for just a few hours. In work he could finally stop being himself...and then he could live and breathe easily. Finally.

He could forget the women who haunted him. All of them.

Chapter 6

Shannon McCabe looked out the window of her apartment and thought about running over to her brother's neighborhood and then immediately ditched the idea. She'd already been by there a couple of times this month.

"Stupid thing to do," she told the ginger-colored cat that was curling its way around her right leg. "I'm twenty-two, an adult, so why do I do those things, do you suppose, Pocket?"

The cat ignored her and kept at its game. Not that it mattered. She knew why she had been going there lately.

He'd sent her a check, and it had been a long time since he had sent one. Her heart broke at the thought that he even bothered to try to help her anymore. Seth had always been so caring. He'd been forced to be responsible for her ungrateful little self when he was barely old enough to be responsible for his own welfare. And she had fought him all the way. She had scratched and bit and complained and cussed and ultimately run. In the end, she had hurt him in the worst way.

The memory of those months of living on the street, the degrading things she'd said and done and had done to her still affected her every move almost three years later. And then, of course, there was the other, the medical thing, the no-baby-ever thing.

Her heart hurt at the thought. She was damaged physically beyond repair. Seth knew that. She was sorry that he knew, because it hurt him. One more thing she would pay for all of her life. Not that Seth knew all she had done and learned while she was living on the streets. Thank goodness.

"We can't ever let him know the full extent of my sins, Pocket," she said. "I almost destroyed Seth, I think. So, like always, I sent the check back. I won't let him take responsibility for me, either financially or emotionally anymore. He did enough when I came back, setting me up with a job and therapy and a place to stay. It killed him to see me, every time, too. I could tell, so I'm never subjecting him to my sorry self again, Pocket, and you can take that to the bank."

The cat finally stopped moving and gave a little sympathetic purr. Shannon picked him up and hugged him until he leapt free.

"Okay, be that way. And don't reprimand me for checking up on Seth now and then, okay? He doesn't look happy. His world is so different now than it used to be. I did that, Pocket. So, I have to just look in now and then and make sure he's still breathing. Can't let him see me, though. I always do the wrong thing with Seth. It's just you and me now."

Pocket batted at a bit of feather Shannon had pulled from an old pillow.

"Who do you think that woman is that's been hanging around him, Pocket? Looks like trouble to me. Seth sure as hell doesn't need any more trouble. What do you think we can do about that?"

Pocket glanced toward Shannon. If a cat could frown, this one was frowning.

"Exactly," Shannon said. "We can make sure she keeps her claws out of him. He needs another troublesome female like he needs a knife in the back. Guess I'll have to keep a lookout. Make sure she doesn't cause any problems."

The sun had barely started to show its face when Molly emerged from her building on the way to the bakery several days later. Moving swiftly down the four steps leading from the narrow brick entranceway, she was almost to the sidewalk when she heard a noise behind her.

Her senses went on full alert. She realized how deserted the street was at this hour, and that with a baby in tow, she would not be able to run very fast. Her heart began to thud, to race. Breathing was next to impossible. She whirled.

"You don't even have a porch light turned on. Do you realize how vulnerable that makes you, lady?"

Molly closed her eyes in relief, and then opened them again. Seth was leaning against the building, one foot braced against the brick, and he did not look happy.

She took a long, deep breath. "Seth? Why—"

"Because I walked past your building and I noticed that there is no outside light and there are big shrubs growing close to the building. You work for a bakery. That means you go to work early. In the dark," he said, eyeing the sky. "That's not good. And don't look at me like that. I know this isn't your building, but just because your landlord must be a certified idiot doesn't mean I'm going to put up with it."

She bristled. "I didn't ask you to fight my battles."

"I know, but I also know a few things about you, Molly Delavan. You believe in the innate goodness of people."

"I don't." She thought of her parents; she thought of Kevin, and barely stifled a shiver.

Seth studied her. His eyes narrowed. "Something is scaring you," he said, his voice a near whisper. "Is it me? I knew better than to come here."

Yes, he was scaring her, but not in the way she meant. His grudging concern was scaring her, because it made her warm to him. She knew better than to allow that. She wanted to repay him, so she could feel she was free of all her debts, all her connections. She didn't want more, but there was something about him…no, she wouldn't allow herself to think that way.

"You stopped because you think I'm not doing all I can to keep Ruthie and me safe. I'm not from the city, and I don't know all the ways. I'll concede that. I'll do what I can to change that. Then you can stop worrying about getting involved."

He looked to the side. "That would be best."

"Who was she?" She hadn't meant to ask that.

He tensed, pinioning her with his gaze. "Who?"

Molly shook her head. "I don't know. Whoever made you feel this protective urge toward women."

He didn't speak, his jaw turned to stone, but the look in his eyes, the anguish there…

"No, it doesn't matter. I promise I'll do my best to figure out how to keep Ruthie and me safe. You think I want to be stupid about safety? I want to be strong, to be able to do everything I can to keep us safe without having to ask anyone for help. I have a child, and I would kill for her, die for her, do anything to protect her, but there are things—" she gestured toward the house "—I've never had to worry about things like bushes where people can hide or whether there was an outside light. It was never important before. It is now."

That was the most she would say, but she had to say that much. Because he was right. She needed to educate herself if she was going to protect her baby.

"You trust too much, you know?"

His words made her bristle, because trusting Kevin Rickman was what had gotten her into this predicament. If people like Seth and Ada were still saying that, if she hadn't learned anything...

Molly took a deep breath and squared her shoulders. "You think you know so much. I don't trust everyone."

To her surprise, he smiled a little. All right, maybe she *had* sounded a bit like a petulant child. "You fell right in with Ada and me. You let people come right up to you and beg for money. Who don't you trust?"

Kevin, Kevin, Kevin. The words ran though her head, but no one could know about Kevin, because if her secrets came out, he would find her. Seth might have helped her, but he didn't have the power to help her run from someone with Kevin's determination and connections.

Seth grinned again. "You trust everyone." For a moment he reached out, as if to brush his fingertips across her cheek. Her heartbeat kicked up, the nerve endings in her skin went on full alert. She almost leaned in to meet his fingertips. And then he halted, his hand frozen in midair. He shoved his hand into his pocket. "You do," he said, frowning this time.

"No." She blurted the word out, angry not just at his inference but at her own stupid reaction to his anticipated caress. "I don't trust...reporters." It was true. The reporters had come out of the woodwork after her parents' death. They had dug up her child-star celebrity past, hounded her. It was those stories that Kevin had unearthed, and that was when he had sought her out and started making big plans, plans she hadn't known about. Plans that could exploit and hurt her baby. When she had objected, he had twisted her arm, threatened to take Ruthie when she was born, to use his connections to declare Molly unfit. If the reporters found her now, so would Kevin.

"I don't trust reporters," she repeated.

Seth studied her silently, carefully, his body still, his eyes dark and judgmental as if he was trying to decide if she was making up something to appease him.

He nodded slightly. "So what? Not a real answer, Molly. No one likes reporters."

She shrugged, afraid she might, if pressed, blurt out her secrets.

"I didn't ask you to help me."

"What time do you get off work?" was his only answer.

"Four o'clock."

"I'll be here. Don't go to Ada's today. You cleaned yesterday. Today we make sure your place is safe. I'll show you what to do." His voice was grim and low.

"Why? Why are you doing this for us?"

He stared directly into her eyes. "Because I don't want you—or your baby—on my conscience. Come on." And he pushed off the building and began to walk.

"Where are we going?"

"I'm walking you to work."

She wanted to tell him that she didn't need his escort, but then she looked at him, at how strong and capable he looked as he moved. It had to be a mask, she supposed. He had to be tired. This was normally the time when he was sleeping, and yet here he was helping her again. Something shifted inside of her. Loneliness and need filled her soul. Even if it was only her enforced solitude that was making her long to get close to Seth, it was there nonetheless.

Right now she didn't feel particularly invincible, and Seth knew the city. He would help her, teach her what she absolutely had to know if she was going to stay hidden.

"Once Ruthie and I are all squared away, and I know all I need to about keeping us safe…"

"Then we won't need to meet any longer," he said.

"Yes. That was what I was going to say." It hadn't been, but it was true. That was what she wanted, total independence. Seth would help her achieve that.

"Now I'll owe you more than ever."

He opened his mouth, and she knew he was going to protest.

"You're helping me. Don't tell me I can't help you. I don't have much you would need or want, but I can cook and I can clean. You have to let me." Her voice grew a little thin at the end, and though she was staring straight ahead, she felt his attention light on her.

"You don't want my safety on your head. I don't want to be indebted to any man," she said, her voice tense. "I can't have that." She had no intention of explaining.

He considered that, the silence stretching out.

"All right," he finally said. "Ada will let you in when I'm away. I won't protest. We'll both do what we need to do in order to live with ourselves."

Molly gave a taut nod. "Seth?"

"Yes?"

"Forget I asked about the woman. I do know one thing about living in the city. You don't ask too many questions."

"That doesn't have anything to do with living in the city. It's just me."

"And me," she said firmly. She turned to look at him as she said the words, and the first slivers of the rising sun lit his dark hair and turned his skin to gold. Even with the scars, it was obvious that he had once been a beautiful man. He still was in many ways. He was also the most masculine man she had ever met. A man who looked at her with fire and yet wanted nothing to do with a woman like her. A man with his own secrets.

It was quite possible, she realized, that he had more secrets than she did. She had no clue what he did for a living, and he hadn't offered any information, even though he worked odd hours. He was one mystery inside another. Furthermore, it was obvious that he knew things she didn't. And if she stared into his eyes long enough, she could see things in those dark gray depths, things that made her shiver. He probably knew the ways of pleasure. Not that that could matter.

Because he lived with barriers. And because she lived with fear that kept her isolated. Maybe she would always be running. She hoped for Ruthie's sake that eventually she could settle down and have some sort of a normal life.

A man like Seth would never be part of a normal, settled life. An ache went through her at the thought, both for herself and for him.

"I'll clean and cook," she promised. "I won't bother you when I come over to clean, and I'll do my best to learn all I need to know quickly."

He would help her, and maybe she really could evade Kevin and feel safe one day.

"We'll make sure you're safe," he said as if he had read her mind.

"That sounds like a promise."

He slowly shook his head. "I don't make them. Don't ask me to." But his voice was like a light caress across her skin. Whether he liked it or not, his voice and his body offered a promise of passion to a woman, and probably always would. He would be a dangerous man to get too close to.

Caught up in her thoughts, Molly suddenly realized that she was standing alone on the sidewalk in front of the bakery, and Seth was moving off down the street.

"Seth?" she called.

"I'll be here at four," he called back, but he didn't turn around. Four o'clock.

In less than a day he would return and take her in
hand. For some reason the hours between now and then
seemed very long. And during the day, while she swept,
the sound of the broom swooshing softly across the old
golden wooden floor reminded Molly of a man's hand
stroking a woman's body.

"Aagh! Stop it," she told herself.

"You okay, Ms. Delavan?" Mr. Alex asked her.

"I'm fine," she told him, but it was a lie. She was
starting to let her life and her thoughts get entwined with
a man with dark sexy eyes. A man who was never going
to touch her in this lifetime.

"Which is a darn good thing," she whispered to herself. But still, she swept harder, trying to pretend she
didn't know what time it was.

"What do you mean, she isn't anywhere?" Kevin
barked into the phone.

"I can't find her," the voice on the other end of the
line answered.

"She's not a pro. She doesn't know how to go deep
cover. And by now she has a baby. That makes her more
visible."

"All I'm saying is that I don't have any leads yet."

"Well, get some. Fast. She's been missing too long."

"She might have tried to disguise herself."

"Let her try. A face like that can't be disguised. I
don't care if she dyed her hair, wore thick glasses, got
colored contacts or shaved her head. She's got cheek-

bones you can't miss, a voice that makes her stand out. It's a face that will make money, especially when people find out who she once was. With a little luck, the kid will have the crowd-pleaser face, too. That means more money, tons more. And no money if we don't find them, so if you ever want to be paid…"

"Got it. What are you going to do if we find her?"

"*When* we find her. If you can't do it, I'll find someone else who can. He'll get your share."

"*When* we find her," the other man said. "What are you going to do then?"

"I'm going to use her. And then I'm going to exercise my parental rights and take the kid. I'm entitled. I'll make big bucks, a lot more than I could ever make hauling in and cuffing the scum of the streets. I'll make her sorry that she thought she could just walk away from me."

Kevin smiled into the phone. Oh, yeah, life—and revenge—was going to be good. Getting even with Molly would be sweet.

And nobody was going to stop him.

Seth ran one hand over his jaw as he made his way to the bakery. He hadn't shaved, which wasn't a big deal. Sometimes he did it on purpose, because it helped the image on the street, but today it was just a matter of not being on top of his game. He had gone home after leaving Molly's apartment and written his column, but then sleep had refused to come.

"She hates reporters," he muttered to himself. Not a big deal. Half the world hated reporters, and everyone seemed to have reasons for doing so. Molly hadn't given him a reason. He couldn't help but wonder what she was hiding, and it was pretty obvious that she was hiding something. Women that looked like her didn't just show up out of the blue around here, did they?

He tried to blank out his mind. She wasn't one of his subjects. Still, she had no idea that he was the very thing she loathed. For a minute he thought of his sister. Shannon loathed him, as well, but she had good reasons for that.

"This is different. I won't let anything happen to her." And he knew it wasn't his sister he was thinking about.

"But don't get the idea you'll ever be a hero, buddy," he told himself. "You're not the type. You just do what has to be done, and then…"

Then he would get the hell away from Molly. He would move deeper into the streets if he had to, stay there longer, live there day and night if need be.

He would do that now, cut all thoughts of her pretty brown eyes and her innocent bravado right out of his world. But not yet. Right now she was alone, a predator's dream, and there wasn't any superhero to come save her.

There was only him, such as he was. What a joke, what a mistake, what the hell was he doing out on the street at this time of day? Yeah, it was going to start getting dark soon, but not the dead-of-night kind he was used to, the dark where people locked their doors, afraid to come out. The people wandering around now were still bright and busy and full of purpose. This wasn't his world anymore.

"Deal with it," he muttered as he leaned against the building next door to the bakery.

And then she came through the door.

She saw him, smiled at him, her brightness chasing away the looming shadows, and he knew he was in major trouble. He'd dealt with knife attacks, gangs, drug dealers and thieves. That kind of fear didn't begin to compare to the fear he felt when he looked into Molly's eyes and his whole body responded.

Thieves were easy. You just kicked some butt, and they ran. But what did you do when a woman like this looked at you as if you were something you were not, something special?

You tamped down that desire rising in your gut, and you did what you came to do.

"Ready for some serious home-protection strategies?" he asked.

She nodded. "Teach me everything you know about…everything," she said, and it was all he could do not to close his eyes and groan.

Chapter 7

"Keep the door open."

Molly blinked at Seth's command.

"Rule number one—don't let a strange man into your apartment. Rule number two—even if you trust a man, an open door means that someone might hear you if you called." He gave her the look, the one that brooked no argument.

Reluctantly she nodded. She watched him as he traversed the limited space of her apartment, running his fingers over locks, examining doors.

"You need a better viewer, one with a wider angle," he said. "With this one, you might see one guy while another one hides off to the side." He frowned when he said it, and she shivered at the thought.

He glanced at her, not missing a thing. "I'm sorry, but—"

"Don't be sorry. You're only telling me what I need to know, but somehow I doubt my landlord is going to let me start installing fixtures in his house."

"He's getting free improvements. He won't argue."

Maybe he was right. Molly couldn't imagine anyone arguing with Seth when he glowered. He moved with cool precision through her apartment, those alert gray eyes not missing a thing.

She blinked when he had given her mailbox a long look and then passed by without mentioning the fact that there was no name on the box. It wasn't the first time someone around here had noted and then ignored her anonymity. When she had rented the apartment, she had paid in cash, and although her landlord gave her a hard stare, he didn't say anything. She had a feeling that references weren't an issue in this part of town.

Still, she had her arguments ready for Seth just in case. She didn't need a mailbox because she wouldn't get any mail. She gave the landlord her payments directly. Utilities were included in the rent. She didn't have any need for a telephone. She wouldn't tell him the truth, which was that she felt safer and less accessible without a mailbox and a telephone, even if it was false security.

"Molly?" Seth said, and she gave him her full attention.

"Is it bad? Have I been putting Ruthie in danger?" she asked.

He smiled slightly. "Not so bad, and I know you would never intentionally endanger her. You just need a few things, a timer for your lights when you're out, the viewer, an outside light, a better lock. I'll take care of it while you're at work tomorrow and trim back the bushes so that there are no significant hiding places. Thugs tend to be opportunists. They hit the easy places. We won't make it easy."

Looking up at him, gratitude rushed through her. For a minute she stepped closer. He leaned toward her.

A sense of longing flowed through her. Heat suffused her body. His eyes grew dark and fierce, and for a moment she thought she might do anything, endure anything just to touch her fingertips to his chest, to have him slide his palm against her waist. But then he took a step back.

Biting her lip, she fought for composure. "Thank you," she said. "Those things you're fixing for me, you'll need supplies. I'll just get my purse." She turned to find it.

He touched her then, his warm hand closing around her arm. His grasp was firm and commanding, but not tight. She could break free easily enough if she wanted to.

She didn't want to. Because I'm alone, she told herself. Because I'm running and not likely to have any human contact anytime soon. But the fact that she wanted it so badly told her that she shouldn't allow the contact. "My purse is over there," she said, even though she wasn't sure it was.

"I'll take care of things, Molly."

"I can't let you pay. These are my expenses. I need to be in charge of my existence, my debts."

"All right." He slowly released her. "But wait until I have receipts to give you. Is that acceptable?"

"I suppose. Is it acceptable for me to come bring dinner and straighten up your place tomorrow night?"

His eyes darkened. She was pretty sure he was going to argue.

She crossed her arms. "We had a deal. If you're going to help me, let me help, too. My self-esteem is suffering enough."

Suddenly he backed away completely. "I'll clear out long enough for you to do that."

A tiny slice of disappointment shot through her. She axed it right then and there. He was right. If just having his hand on her arm filled her with longing for more of his touch, being in an apartment together wouldn't be smart. She had already exercised bad judgement with Kevin. It wouldn't happen twice.

He turned to go. "When I'm done, no one will be able to get in here," he told her. "Not even me."

Unless one day she opened the door and invited him in, she couldn't help thinking. Surely she wouldn't be that foolish, would she? Kevin had at least seemed like any other man, a harmless man, when she had met him.

Seth wasn't harmless. She could tell that every time she looked into his eyes. He was a man who could make a woman weak. And being weak was dangerous.

"Well, we'll be done soon, anyway. It won't matter," she told herself after he was gone.

Molly was almost to Seth's building the next day when she got an eerie feeling that seemed to settle right between her shoulder blades. She turned and looked behind her, but there was no one on the street.

Ruthie Ann blew out a noisy bubble.

"Yes, sweetie, Mom *is* probably overreacting. I'm seeing the boogeyman behind every tree, but you know what Seth and Ada say. You can't be too careful. Better to look like an idiot glancing over my shoulder than to get caught."

Ruthie leaned back in the chest carrier and smiled at her mother. Molly's heart lurched.

"I love you, too, angel. Don't ever doubt that. I'll take extraspecial care of you."

But as she concentrated on her child, that someone's-watching-you feeling came to her again. Molly's heart pounded. She kept walking and then, holding Ruthie tight and whirling as fast as she could, she did a one-eighty.

There was a woman. A blond blur. That was all she had time to register before the woman slipped down a side street and disappeared from sight.

"Not Kevin," she whispered to herself as she waited for relief to flood through her and for her knees to regain some semblance of stability.

Not Kevin, and yet…someone who didn't want to be seen. Someone he had sent to look for her?

"No." I won't believe that. Not yet. The woman was probably just a druggie looking to lift some money. Still dangerous, though.

"Better get you inside, pumpkin." She rushed to Ada's building and let herself in.

"Go on up. Here's the key," Ada said when Molly explained that Seth had given her permission to enter his apartment. "Can't believe he let you do this. That boy doesn't let anyone inside. Is there something you two aren't telling me?"

"I'm cleaning, Ada. That's all." But as she turned over Ruthie and trooped upstairs, a small bag of groceries in one hand, some cleaning supplies in the other, Molly stopped outside Seth's door and breathed in deeply.

On this side of the door, she had no connections to the man who lived here. Once she walked inside, she would know more of him, and knowing too much of Seth was probably unwise.

Still, she had asked for this, so carefully opening the door, she stepped inside and looked around.

A small trace of disappointment slid through her. The room was almost bare. But then, what had she expected?

Even the pictures she had glimpsed that one day were gone. The room didn't look as if it needed much cleaning.

Still, she put the groceries away and went through the motions of dusting and vacuuming the living room and cleaning the kitchen and bathroom.

Moving toward a door that must lead to Seth's bedroom, Molly felt her breathing kick up a notch, but when she turned the knob, the door didn't open.

"Okay, so the barriers are up," she whispered. And why not? She had barriers of her own. But if the man wouldn't let her really clean his place, how was she helping him?

Molly smiled. "Nice try, Seth. No color in your life? Don't think that's going to fly with me."

She moved into the kitchen. Soon the air was filled with the scent of baking lasagna and garlic bread. A salad sat waiting in the fridge, and a small plate of Mr. Alex's cookies.

"I should have brought a centerpiece, something bright to add some color. Next time…" she whispered, and then stopped. "Or maybe this time."

Taking a deep breath, she opened a cabinet. Surely there was something here she could use. She peered into the back of the cabinet. Her mouth curved upward.

"They're just kitchen cabinets," she reasoned. "Not a place anyone keeps private stuff. And this will do." She reached in. In only minutes she had set everything up and left the apartment, clicking the lock closed behind her. The sound echoed, emphasizing the lack of human company.

A profound sense of loneliness assaulted Molly as she moved down the stairs. She picked up her daughter from Ada and cuddled her.

She had Ruthie. All she needed was Ruthie. Who

cared that the man who lived upstairs wanted so little to do with her that he left the house while she was there?

"You fix him up?" Ada asked.

"I did what I could."

"Um, well with Seth, that's the most any of us can say."

"He doesn't have anyone?"

Ada flicked on the television set. "You have the sweetest baby ever born. You know that?" she asked, ignoring Molly's question.

Molly got the picture. "She's a gift." She murmured the words into her daughter's fuzzy blond curls.

Ada grunted. "Good that you know that. Don't ever let anything come between you and her. Bad things happen when family doesn't stay together." And again, Molly wondered about Ada and about Seth. And, though she tried to push the bad thoughts away, she remembered that despite everything she tried to do, there was a man set on coming between her and her child.

A man she had once planned on marrying. Maybe Seth was right. Maybe this keeping-their-distance stuff was right.

"Is Seth usually gone at this time of day?" she ventured.

Shaking her head, Ada grinned. "No, Seth rarely goes out at this time of day."

"So I chased him away?"

"He could have stayed."

"I think I make him uncomfortable," Molly ventured.

Ada cackled. "I think you make him remember he's a man, and he doesn't like that at all."

Neither did she, Molly thought as she made her way home. But then she remembered Seth's dark eyes studying her. She remembered how her whole body had responded when he had simply touched her arm. All right, sometimes she liked remembering that Seth was a man. It was a devil of a thought, but…

"Better to know your devils, Ruthie," she told her child, "so you can either run or stand and deliver right away." If she had known Kevin was a devil, she would have run.

But then she wouldn't have Ruthie, would she?

There were no easy answers sometimes. With Seth there would probably never be any. She wouldn't get a Ruthie out of this one.

"Remember that," she told herself and the baby. "Some men will only break your heart. Stay away and be happy if they tell you no. It's a blessing to be unwanted."

So the little part of her that longed to rub up against Seth McCabe's chest had just better settle back down and be quiet.

"Is she gone?" Seth asked, stepping out from the sectioned-off third of the basement where the storage bins and laundry tubs took up space.

"She's gone," Ada grumbled. "Aren't you ashamed? A grown man hiding from a pretty little thing like that?"

"Don't give me that crap, Ada. She's alone in the world. She's afraid…of something or someone. I don't know of who or what, and frankly, it's none of my business. I don't want to butt into her business. But I do know this—she doesn't need to be closed up in a small apartment with a man towering over her and making her uncomfortable."

"If she's alone maybe she needs a friend."

"I don't do friendship."

Ada snorted. "Now you're the one talking crap. You help me all the time. That's friendship or I don't know what is."

"You're old. You need help," he said with a grin.

"And so does she."

"And so does she," he agreed, "but she doesn't always want to admit it."

"Sounds like someone I know."

"Think what you like. I don't think it's a good idea for me to hang around when Molly is here."

"Because she makes you itch to touch."

He didn't deny it. "A man is not what she needs in her life right now. She just had a baby."

"Yes, and taking care of that baby is probably good for her. Taking care of you and me probably would be, too. But nobody likes to do things for someone without a little positive feedback."

"I'll thank her when I see her. On the street or here, in the hallway. Not in my place."

"Must be lonely being alone most of the time with

no one to talk to. No one who can talk back, at any rate."
She gave him a pointed look. "At least you, antisocial
as you are, can come talk to me when you start to feel
like you have to say something to someone other than
the walls."

Okay, she had him there, Seth conceded. Solitude
was a blessing in many ways, but there were days…

"All right," he said. "I might stay in my room when
she's here. I'll work. If she needs to say something, I'll
be right on the other side of the door."

He gave Ada a hard stare. She stared back and
opened her mouth.

"No, I am not going to become friendly with Molly,"
he said, holding up a hand. "Don't even think about it,
Ada. It's not meant to be. This isn't one of your television shows."

"The people on my shows have more sense than you
do."

"Most likely."

"As long as you don't avoid her so much she feels
like a pariah."

"I said I'd stay."

"Promise?"

"Don't push it, Ada. I told you yes. I don't go back
on my word once it's given."

Suddenly Ada smiled. "That's better than I hoped for.
I was just thinking you might come out of the basement
and say goodbye to her when she left."

He swore.

"Seth," she admonished.

"You deserved that, Ada. And don't tell me that wasn't you I heard swearing at the furnace the other day."

"Darn furnace," she agreed. "A woman alone has a heavy load to bear."

"You know I'd fix it for you if you asked."

"I know. You're a good man, Seth."

"No. I'm not, but I'll play your party games with Molly if you think it will do any good."

"She's pretty, isn't she?"

"Ada."

"Just saying. I wish I could remember where I've seen her."

"You haven't. Now go watch your show. I'm going back upstairs. I have some work to do and I have to eat before I go out."

She nodded and started toward the stairs.

"What are you doing?"

His landlady glanced back over her shoulder. "You think I'm not going to go up and see what she did? I'm nosy, you know."

He did know. He also knew that when it counted, she controlled her tendencies. "Okay, we're just talking a little cleaning and cooking. No major big deal."

But when he threw open the door and he and Ada looked in, the delicious scent of pasta and garlic bread drifted out.

As if drawn by the scent, they both stepped inside, and then Seth noticed that the table was set with blue-

and-white dishes he hadn't seen in years. There was a centerpiece of small pink-and-blue glass circus animals, marching around a round blue place mat. The animals had been Shannon's. There was a crystal glass from the set that his mother had washed and put away lovingly many times and which he hadn't wanted to ever see again. All things he had thrown in the back of a kitchen cupboard years ago and refused to look at.

His heart started to thud. His throat felt as if it would close up. If he hadn't leaned against the wall he might have fallen, his knees buckling beneath him.

He must have made a sound, because Ada turned to him, and he was pretty sure that she got a good look at his face as he stared at the table decorations before he managed to beat back his reaction.

"Ada," he said carefully. "Do you have any cardboard boxes?"

"Yeah, I'll get 'em." She turned to go.

He stayed her with his hand. "No, you tell me where. I'll get them. And then…I'll bring the food down to your place. We'll share."

He turned to go.

"I don't claim to understand, but I can see mistakes were made. She was just trying to make a place for you, bring some color in here," Ada said, motioning to his apartment.

He took a deep, shuddering breath. "I know that. It's not her fault that I'm like this."

"So…"

Seth turned and gave Ada a long, serious look. "I gave my word, Ada. I'm not going to make her feel uncomfortable, but I'm not going to start anything with her, either. Believe me when I say that that would be the very worst thing in the world for her."

Ada looked down at his clenched fists. She glanced toward the seemingly innocent collection of dishes and trinkets on the table. Then she slowly nodded.

"Yes, I see. You may be right about that. I'll…should I talk to her for you?"

"No. That won't be necessary. I'll do what has to be done. She'll never know that anything was wrong."

Chapter 8

Something was wrong, Molly thought when she entered Seth's apartment the next evening. Ada had gone out and left the key for her, so she had Ruthie with her when she opened Seth's door.

The living room was as empty as it had been the day before. The dishes she had brought had been cleaned and left on the counter, but nothing much had changed, other than the fact that he had already set the table. A plain white plate, a functional glass, a paper napkin. The adorable animal figures and the pretty china were nowhere in sight, but that wasn't what had Molly pricking up her ears.

There was music coming from behind Seth's bedroom door. He must have left it on…or else he was here.

The very thought made her heart start to race like some silly young girl with her first crush. Of course, that was what it was like. Hero worship just because the man had helped her. He had also warned her away, and he was right.

She would ignore him. If he was actually here, that is.

Shaking her head, Molly laid a pink-and-white fluffy blanket down on the floor and set Ruthie up in her own little spot. Then she began cutting up vegetables for soup.

The music wafted through the door. Grieg, she guessed. Without thought, she hummed a bit.

Something crashed to the floor in the other room.

Molly sucked in a breath. What had happened? Was he hurt? And if he wasn't, what would he think if she started beating on his door?

But the music stopped and the silence set in, and then she began to worry in earnest.

She should ignore her fears. They were probably all wrong.

But all she could hear was the sound of the clock on the wall and Ruthie's baby noises.

Molly tentatively moved toward Seth's door. She raised one fist to knock, then stopped midair. Think, think, Molly, she told herself. Things are different now. You only have yourself to rely on. You have to make wise decisions. Meeting up with Seth in a bedroom couldn't be wise.

But leaving him when he might be hurt would surely drive her insane. What good would wisdom do then?

"Seth," she called, tapping lightly on the door. "I— I heard something fall. Are you all right?"

The door swung open wide, and there he was standing tall and cool before her. Looking infinitely capable, as if nothing could hurt him. What had she been thinking, wondering if he had been hurt just because she heard a little noise? He obviously hadn't wanted to see her. If he had, he would have come out when she first entered the apartment.

"I'm…sorry," she said, lifting one shoulder. "Of course you're fine."

He dipped his head slightly. "No problem." But his voice sounded a bit tight. She had been standing so close to the door that when he opened it she had taken a step forward to keep her balance. Now, her eyes were on a level with Seth's chest, and she had to tilt her head back to see his face. Doing so made her feel vulnerable and small. She couldn't help remembering how he had carried her and sheltered her that first night, sharing the warmth of his body with her.

Suddenly breathing was difficult. She raked her teeth over her bottom lip nervously.

His eyes narrowed. She almost thought he leaned slightly, too, but that couldn't be right, could it? He didn't even want her here. And that thought was enough to send her scooting backward. She was blocking the only way out of his room, essentially holding him captive.

"I'll just finish making your dinner," she said.

"You don't have to do that."

"We had a deal." She tried to look stern.

For a minute she thought he was going to smile. But he simply said, "All right."

Busying herself at the stove, she could hear him moving behind her, pacing. He probably wished she would just go, and she...well, she was so very aware of him.

The silence was like a living, breathing beast in the room, the spoon she was using clinking loudly against the pan, Seth's footsteps heavy against the linoleum. Suddenly Ruthie cooed, a small, bright sound.

Seth's footsteps stopped.

Molly turned. Her baby was on her back, her little hands opening and closing. She was smiling, and there was no doubt that she was looking straight at Seth.

His face had turned pale, the scars standing out more vividly, his eyes dark with...something, perhaps pain?

Ruthie continued smiling and cooing. She reached up as if she would touch him even though they were six feet apart.

Seth tensed, like a man facing his own demise. Something wasn't right. He obviously didn't like babies.

"I'm sorry," Molly said, putting down her spoon and moving to Ruthie, planning on picking up her.

"No. Don't." Seth's voice was very low and raspy.

Molly looked at him. He was shaking his head.

"She's just doing what babies do." Which didn't explain at all why he looked as if he had just seen something horrific. "Children should be free to be children." He stepped away.

Molly nodded curtly. Ruthie had gone back to playing with her toes, completely unaware of any drama she had caused.

He was absolutely right, Molly thought. Children should be free to be children, but a man should also not have to feel uncomfortable in his own home. She had come here to do something good for him, not to punish him.

"I want to thank you for what you did at my apartment. I feel much safer now." She smiled at Seth.

"You should get a dog," he said suddenly. "A dog is the best deterrent to intruders. If you get the right one, he'll keep intruders away, keep an eye on the little one and become a companion, too."

"Can't. It's against the rules."

"I'll bet your landlord could be persuaded if he was told that it was a safety issue."

She had to smile. "You're not big on rules, are you?"

Seth shrugged. "Rules have their place. They should be adaptable. You could use a guard dog."

"*You* don't have one."

"I don't have a baby." And never would, she was pretty sure, if his reaction to Ruthie's smile was any indication.

She nodded. "You have a point." And then she simply looked at him. She wanted to do something to let him know how much she appreciated all that he had done for her, yet he seemed not to want anything from her. It almost seemed that the best thing she could do for him would be to leave him alone.

Her heart hurt at that admission. Silly but true. She *should* leave him alone. What if Kevin found her and what if he found out that Seth had been helping her. She could be putting Seth in danger.

"I'll let you get back to what you were doing." She tipped her head toward his bedroom. "I'll try not to be here too long."

He turned to go. And then he turned back.

"Thank you for the help...and the food. It was delicious."

Foolishly her heart began to sing. Tears stung at the back of her eyes. How silly. It was just a small and grudging compliment. But she was alone, and this man had made a difference in her solitude.

She looked toward the table. "I could do more," she ventured. "Add some color?"

"No," he said swiftly. "Yesterday...the decorations. That was nice, but..."

"But not like you." She realized that even as she said the words out loud. Of course. What was a man like Seth McCabe doing with a set of blown-glass animals?

"Not like me," he agreed. "And..." For a moment she thought he was going to close his eyes. "And nice." He repeated the word with some resignation. "But not necessary."

"I'm sorry," she stammered. "You don't like color."
She felt awkward and stupid and wrong.

And then he stepped forward. He put his hand on her
shoulder. His touch was like fire, like something she had
wanted all her life and not known. She resisted that
feeling and looked up at him.

His eyes were like dark flames, too. "You're so
wrong," he whispered. "I like color, but those animals...I just can't have them."

"They're not yours," she said.

"No. I've put them away, but I appreciate the
thought."

She nodded.

"I have to work now," he said.

"Yes. You work at night," she said, half to herself.
"What...what do you do?"

"I work," he said, and then he slipped away, back into
his room, where he turned the music loud.

I work, she thought. That was it, all he would share.
Shouldn't she be getting the picture? He was a man who
had all kinds of secrets. He was also a man who didn't
want to be near her and who looked at a baby as if she
could destroy him.

And she was a woman who had gotten involved with
a man she thought she knew but who had turned out to
be a scary stranger.

Shouldn't she be learning her lesson by now? Wasn't
it clear that she should run from Seth, just as he wanted
her to?

But in the back of her mind as she finished the dinner, picked up her child and trooped down the stairs, she heard him: *Children should be allowed to be children; you need a dog to protect you.*

"Everything about him shouts 'run away,' Molly," she whispered to herself as she moved toward Ada's apartment. "So why aren't you running? And what would it take to unlock Seth's doors?"

Then she knocked on the door of the only person who was likely to know the answer to that question.

Seth listened long after Molly's footsteps had progressed down the stairs. She was probably stopping in to see Ada, but then she would step back out on the streets, headed for home.

In the dark.

He swore beneath his breath. What was she doing on the streets at this time of night, anyway? He sniffed and breathed in the spices emanating from the kitchen.

"She's cooking and cleaning for you, you idiot," he said, answering his own question. "And if she gets hurt going home, if anything happens to her, it will be on your head."

But she wouldn't get hurt. Because he would be right behind her. Wandering outside around here probably wasn't the smartest thing he'd ever done, especially since he usually didn't hit the streets until several hours later when most of the foot traffic had dropped to nil.

A man with his scarred face stood out, like it or not. It wouldn't do to be noticed too much.

But there were innocents abroad. Like it or not, someone had to make sure they made it home safely. And really, who paid much attention to what happened in this part of town, anyway? The wealthy didn't care, and there were other places that were more likely haunts for those who wanted to rip someone off, walk away with something good and get away quickly.

Following Molly home probably wasn't that much of a risk to his cover. He thought of her trusting brown eyes, that pretty smile she turned on him too often. And he knew that, whatever the risks, he would take them. He was no hero and didn't want to be, but if anything happened to her and that baby...

"Heaven help the man who touches her," he said.

He said the words, knowing he had uttered similar words in the past...and he had failed. It had nearly killed him. It *had* killed his relationship with his sister.

"So don't fail," he told himself. "And don't think about her. Just follow her home and then get out, back to where you belong."

Which was nowhere. He belonged nowhere.

"And don't want to, either," he reminded himself.

He sat down to eat his dinner and to wait for Molly to head home.

Chapter 9

Ada put down the copy of the newspaper she had been reading, ushered Molly into her apartment, then reached out and took Ruthie into her arms.

"'Mean Streets' again?"

Ada nodded. "That Nick Dawson is one great reporter."

Molly tried to suppress her shiver. "I haven't read him, but I've seen too many bad reporters to ever like one."

"In person?" Ada raised a brow.

Molly's breathing hitched. Bad move, Delavan, she thought. "Haven't you seen the way reporters always stick their microphones in grief-stricken relatives' faces?"

"Oh, that," Ada said with a shrug. "That's different. Nick tells it like it is. He knows Chicago. He *is* the city."

"Maybe." But Molly had trouble injecting any enthusiasm into her voice. If a reporter ever found out that she was hiding here…she grew sick at the thought.

Fortunately, Ruthie burbled at that moment. "Aren't you something, sweetie," Ada cooed. "I'll bet you thought we forgot you were there. As if we could."

Ruthie blew another bubble and smiled.

Ada gazed at the baby as if she had just done something monumental. "You're a doll, aren't you?" she asked. Then, without looking up, she said, "He didn't throw you out, did he?"

Molly didn't even have to think about what Ada meant. "Seth wouldn't do that." But that didn't mean he was ever happy to see her.

"Not physically, but that boy can put up some pretty serious barriers."

Which was as good a lead-in as any, Molly figured.

"I'm not sure I'm not doing more harm than good by going there," she admitted.

"I'm not the person to ask."

"Who is?"

Ada stared at her. "You've got a point. Seth is good at hiding his reactions to things, so sometimes—heck, most times—it's hard to tell what he's thinking."

"He…must have had a hard life."

"You mean the scars? I don't know much about that

other than the fact that he lost his parents in a fire eight years ago when he was nineteen."

Molly barely hid her gasp. "He told you that?"

"I'm his landlady. I don't rent to just anyone. Some guy comes to you looking like he goes around beating up on people and being beat up, you want to know that he's not going to be a problem. He told me about the fire, reluctantly, just the basics. He wasn't there when it started. He tried to save them, but he couldn't. I don't know much more than that. But I can tell you this. It killed him losing his parents like that. He cared more than he wants to admit, and that's why I didn't even press him to talk to me about the knife marks. He might have owed me some explanation, but he doesn't owe me his soul. I know enough now, and I know he won't harm you or Ruthie."

Molly was having trouble breathing. The pain Seth must have gone through—had she ever really thought he would hurt her? "I know Seth isn't a risk to my child, Ada. He saved our lives. What I don't know is whether I'm causing him grief by pushing myself into his life and trying to repay him this way, but I don't know any other way. I don't want to make him uncomfortable."

"Hon, he's a man with a past, but he's also blunt. If you get to be too much of a nuisance, he'll tell you so. I ought to know. He lives in my building, but he lets me know when I've gone too far or pushed too hard." She chuckled.

"Do you push too hard with Seth often?" Molly asked, not bothering to hide a smile.

"As much as I can, Molly. Wouldn't hurt for you to push him a little, too. Seth needs to get knocked out of his routines and onto his butt now and then. He needs to be a part of the living."

"I'll keep that in mind," Molly said as she gathered Ruthie and prepared to go. But she knew that she didn't want to shake Seth up too much, because every time they got too close, she was the one who ended up shaky and confused and aching. Now that she knew Seth had a tragic history, that made him doubly dangerous. People with histories built solid walls to protect themselves. She knew, because she was very busy building her own walls. And she was afraid Seth could topple them with just a look.

Out on the streets, Jeff Payton wandered. He looked into the eyes of every homeless man he met. He studied the torn bits of newspaper one man was using as a blanket.

"How ironic that they use the 'Mean Streets' column to stay warm." But not that ironic. "Mean Streets" had opened the eyes of everyday citizens to what happened out here. It chronicled the plight of those who were too ill to live on the pavement but had no money to go anywhere else, their illness preventing them from working, their lack of work leaving them with no insurance to cover a doctor's care. The column spoke of the chronic homeless, the families who were temporarily down on their luck and demoralized by the business of not having a place for their children to stay. It spoke of the teen-agers who worked the streets, learning things they should only be reading about in the papers, and yes, the column dealt with the violence, the fact that some felt that those who lived on the streets didn't deserve to exist.

Who in the hell wrote that stuff?

Jeff stared into the vacant eyes of a man huddled against the curb, the holes in his lightweight coat little protection against the elements. The city's leaders tried to provide shelter and food on cold nights and bring people in out of the elements, but many didn't want to come in. He supposed they had their reasons, and the column attempted to sort out those reasons.

But who wrote the column? There was no record of Nick Dawson.

"Whoever he is, he has to be a chameleon."

Jeff hadn't mastered that art yet. Everyone he passed looked at him with wary, suspicious eyes.

"I'm never going to find my subject this way. I'm missing something here," he whispered to himself. "Something vital. What would it take to draw out the writer? What clues are there that I'm not seeing?"

No matter, whoever the unknown writer was, sooner or later, he or she would make a mistake.

"Then I'll know. I'll have a story that will get the attention of readers everywhere," he said. "So think, man, think. If I were the author of the column and I didn't live on the streets full-time, where would I be the rest of the time? Somewhere convenient to the homeless hot spots, undoubtedly. And how would I get in and out without being noticed? Find the answer to those questions, Payton," he told himself, "and you're halfway there."

The next day Seth waited until it was quiet in his living room. No baby sounds or even the sound of Molly's footsteps on his kitchen linoleum emitted from the other room.

"What a coward you are," he told himself. Hiding from a woman and a baby this way, locking himself up with his computer. But he remembered another baby with pretty blond curls, a winning smile and adoration written all over her face every time she'd looked at him. That is, until after the death of their parents when he had taken on the task of being father and mother to her and had botched things so badly. Her smiles had disappeared. Then she had disappeared. When he finally got her back, she no longer smiled.

He didn't want to be responsible for anyone's smiles anymore. So he waited until Molly had gone. She'd shown up this day with a ton of cleaning supplies, obviously planning on tackling the places she hadn't touched before. He'd seen her coming down the street, and he had retreated.

Coward, he thought again, but that, after all, was just a word and what could words do to him? Words weren't death. Words weren't a young girl's dreams crushed before she'd barely been old enough to have dreams, and words, though he made his living with them, weren't redemption. They couldn't change the past, even though he hoped they could change the future. Which was why he wrote. But he'd been sitting here for hours, and today the words hadn't come.

Besides, she was gone. He could breathe a bit now.

Seth opened the door…and found Molly sitting on the shapeless tan couch in his living room.

She looked up at him with wide brown eyes.

"What the hell—"

She shook her head frantically, nodding toward the floor. Ruthie lay on a blue blanket, her fist tucked into her mouth, her long lashes against her cheeks. She curled around herself in sleep. Relaxed. Had he ever been that relaxed?

Maybe many years ago…

He turned back to Molly. She met his eyes warily, guilt practically seeping out of her. He recognized the look.

"Molly?" he asked, his voice very low to keep from waking her child. "What's wrong?"

She shook her head. "Nothing." But one hand was half tucked beneath her, a torn and dusty piece of paper in her grasp. Her fingers clenched and unclenched as if she didn't know what to do with the paper. A pale rose stain suffused her cheeks.

He glanced at the paper again and saw what it was.

Half of the check his sister had sent back to him and that he thought he had thrown away. Part of it must have missed the garbage can and ended up in some cob-webbed corner.

To her credit, she didn't look away or try to make excuses when he returned his gaze to her. She stared directly into his eyes, even though he could tell she would have liked to run.

"Aren't you going to ask me about it?" he asked.

She didn't say anything for a moment, then she swallowed hard. "Would you tell me if I asked?"

He didn't even have to think. "Absolutely not."

"Then I'm not going to ask."

"Good." He started to move toward the door, except...there she was, looking like shame was eating her up. But she had nothing to be ashamed of. He did.

Seth knelt before her. Gently he started to pry the piece of paper from her fingers. She opened her palm and let go. When she did, his fingertips brushed her skin. A low ache went through him, a terrible, strong and relentless ache.

He couldn't seem to help himself. His gaze went to hers and what he saw there was like a pounding in his chest. If he wanted to, he could touch her right now. He could taste her lips. She would let him.

And that all but killed him. Swiftly he rose, moved to the door and out into the hall, headed for the street. On any other day, he wouldn't be going out yet. It was far too early.

But he couldn't stay there with her now. Because for a moment there, staring into her eyes, eyes that knew what pain was all about, eyes that didn't look at him as if he was what he knew he was, he had wanted to do more than just touch her. He had wanted to tell her everything.

The thought nearly made him stumble. He couldn't think of anything he could do that would be worse or more destructive. If he told her even one thing, the little control that kept him together would unravel and someone would end up getting hurt.

He didn't want her to be around when that happened.

So, once again, he was out before full dark had fallen. This was getting to be a bad habit, maybe even a dangerous habit. If he didn't watch out, he would blow his cover, and if he did that…if he did that…well, he just didn't know.

The "Mean Streets" column was all that enabled him to move forward in life, to feel that he still had something good to offer the world, that he could still make some small difference. If he lost it through carelessness or through misplaced lust, what would he become?

Molly began to gather up her things, her fingers shaking. When Seth had touched her, she had never felt such longing…or such desire. And the look in his eyes when he had seen what she was holding…what did it mean?

For that matter, who was Shannon McCabe?

Ada had said that Seth lost his parents, but had they been all the family he had? Was Shannon his mother's name or was she that blond girl in the picture? Maybe she was a cousin, an aunt?

She didn't know, but one thing was certain. Whoever Shannon McCabe was, she meant something to Seth, something painful, because the look in his eyes when he had seen the torn strip of check in her hand had been anguished. That was his signature on the check, yet it had been torn in half. What did that mean?

"None of your business, Delavan," she told herself. But she wanted to do something meaningful for him, and maybe if she knew who this Shannon was...

"No," she said, her movements becoming more purposeful. "He wouldn't want that." Just as she knew he would never want to know what she had felt when his fingertips had stroked her skin.

Molly groaned. I wish we hadn't touched, she thought. But she knew she lied.

Shannon McCabe watched the pretty brown-haired woman coming out of Seth's building carrying a baby. It was the same woman she'd seen around here before, even though she didn't appear to actually live in the building.

"So what's the deal?" she asked the wind. "Not a salesperson. She certainly isn't dressed for that part, and besides, she's got that baby with her all the time."

Shannon's heart stumbled at the thought of the baby.

She forced herself to push past the pain and think about her target, the woman. True, all her information wasn't firsthand. She couldn't afford to come around here very often. Too much likelihood that Seth might spot her. That wouldn't be good.

But she knew the streets and she had her sources. The word was that the woman had been here almost every day this past week. The word also was that the woman had no past and was constantly looking over her shoulder.

Shannon had known a lot of people like that and most of them weren't good.

"So watch yourself, lady," she said, her eyes following the woman down the street. "Because I'm watching you."

Not that she would do too much or pry. Wasn't that the sin she had always accused Seth of when he was trying to raise her? She had taunted him with it and done all she could to make him back off and hate her and leave her alone. "Get out of my face," she'd told him time and time again.

A sharp pain at the memory and all that had followed rolled through her. She fought it off. It was an old acquaintance, anyway, and she deserved every stabbing regret. Life had never been the same since. She couldn't go back and rewrite history.

But she could continue to watch her brother's back… a little. She could keep making sure the woman with the baby didn't cause him any grief.

When the woman's footsteps faded into the distance, Shannon turned to leave. She heard the sliding scrape of a shoe on cement, but no one was there.

Ordinarily that would be a good thing. She would leave it alone. But this was different. She'd been watching Seth and maybe someone else had, too. Maybe someone associated with that woman who'd been hanging around.

So Shannon lightly tiptoed forward as silently as she could. She knew how to do that. She'd been forced to learn.

Quickly she rounded the corner and nearly ran smack into a man, one with chestnut curls and pretty blue eyes.

Those eyes widened as he took her in, giving her a slow once-over from her head to her toes.

She sucked in a breath as her body reacted. Traitor.

"Who are you and what are you doing following me?" she demanded.

The man gave her a crinkly smile. "Sorry, ma'am, for nearly bulldozing you," he said, giving her a slight bow. "My mistake. I was just out for a walk and didn't know you were there."

Then he sauntered away, whistling some unfamiliar but jaunty tune.

"Out taking a walk," she said to herself, her hands on her hips. "My rear end he's just out taking a walk." No man that clean-cut wandered the streets around here. He belonged on Michigan Avenue or in Lincoln Park. There was no way he was a native to this neighborhood.

And what on earth was there to see around here, anyway?

But then she remembered how he had looked her over.

"Well too bad, bucko," she whispered. "This body is not for you." Or for anyone else, for that matter.

Not anymore.

Jeff Payton took his time walking two blocks, whistling all the while, before he ducked into an alley and let his breath out in a whoosh.

"Okay, bud, that was one close call," he said. He had been dogging the guy in the three-story brownstone's footsteps for several days now. Seth McCabe, he thought the man's name was. A total loner, a shadow who normally only came out in the middle of the night. But thanks to the pretty little brown-haired woman, he'd been out on the street during more rational hours lately. He was one of several leads that Jeff had been following in the hopes that he would uncover his quarry.

Not that McCabe was cooperating. So far he hadn't done anything suspicious. He was on the streets only part of the time, but that habit was more common than most people realized. It was only the brown-haired woman who had made Jeff think something was strange about the guy. He'd obviously been helping her. She was cookies-and-cream pretty, even elegant in a well-scrubbed way. McCabe was one scarred-up dude, a guy who looked like he ate knives for lunch and would have no compunction about slipping a knife in your back if you did him wrong. Somehow the two together just didn't fit. And in conversations he'd overheard, it was clear that McCabe was smarter than the average guy hanging out on the street.

In fact, McCabe had been so preoccupied with the woman lately that Jeff had been able to get pretty close once or twice.

Until today.

Who was the cute little blond with the ponytail, the gorgeous body and the don't-try-anything-with-me-buster attitude?

"Don't know, but I'd sure like to know more." And not just because she looked like she'd been scoping out McCabe, too.

What was with Seth McCabe, anyway? He had two beautiful women following him around town.

"Maybe he's just an eccentric," Jeff said, venturing back onto the street and heading for the nearest subway. "Plenty of those around. Maybe he's got money I don't know about, doing the Howard Hughes thing. Or maybe it's something I haven't thought of yet." Whatever Mc-Cabe's game was, it wouldn't hurt to keep the guy in his sights. And those women, too.

Especially the pretty blonde who looked as if she'd like to stick a stiletto in his heart.

That should have sent him packing. Instead it made him want to get to know her better.

Chapter 10

It was *not* any big deal that he was checking up on Molly, Seth told himself as he neared her house the next evening. True, she hadn't come to his house, and true that had him a bit worried, but she was an adult. She had no obligations to him.

Still, as he turned the corner and saw her locking her door, on the point of leaving, a small *whoosh* of relief made his chest feel tight.

"Molly," was all he could manage to say. She looked up.

"Whew, I'm sorry I'm late, but man, it's just been one of those days. I broke a glass, I had trouble getting Ruthie into her sleepers, I couldn't find my key and then…"

She stopped speaking and looked at him. "What are you doing here, anyway?" she finally asked.

He had to grin. He just couldn't help himself, and it was not something he was at all used to doing. Except for a few moments with Ada, he probably hadn't even bothered smiling very much these past few years. But she just looked so…

Flustered, rushed, flushed, sparkling, adorable.

The last thought brought him up cold, hit him somewhere that nearly had him choking and sputtering in denial. Except the thought had already escaped into his consciousness. He tried to muster a frown, then gave it up.

"Molly, it's okay. I was just—well, let's face it, when a person is expected and she doesn't show up around here, you've got to wonder if she's met up with trouble."

She stared at him wide-eyed, her mouth hanging open slightly. Then she smiled, a brilliant smile. "You thought I had been mugged when I was only being completely idiotically disorganized? That's so very nice of you to come check on me. But really, Ruthie and I are fine." She looked down at herself and her baby. "See? Nothing to worry about."

Except that he wasn't fine. In fact, he was starting to look forward to her visits, to watch for her, to worry like mad when she didn't show up on time.

"Damn," he said, then he looked at the baby, the one he tried not to look at too often. "Sorry," he mumbled.

"I'd better wash your mouth out with soap," Molly said with a chuckle. "Next thing you know, Ruthie's first word will be something unrepeatable."

And Seth was so charmed by her laughter that he forgot about all the things he was doing wrong and the fact that he had no right getting this entangled.

"I'll try to watch myself from now on," he said dryly. "I assume you're on your way to Ada's."

"Of course." But in spite of her smiles, he couldn't help noticing that there were hints of dark smudges beneath her eyes, the tiniest droop to her shoulders.

"No," he said. "Not today. You're tired."

"Yes, today. And I'm not that tired."

"Molly…"

"Seth, I think Ada is having her ladies over tomorrow."

"Ada's been having her ladies over twice a week for the past forty years, and she's gotten along just fine without help. Heck, if she needs help, I'm capable."

"Yeah, you'd look real cute wearing an apron with a feather duster in your hand."

"Ada would probably get a charge out of it."

"I'm sure she would, but it's not going to happen, Seth. This is my territory."

And the way she said that, with pride and dignity, gave him reason to believe that she needed a few things to call her own. Nevertheless…

"You can be ruler of Ada's palatial estate and dust her Marilyn Monroe statuettes tomorrow. Today just rule your own roost. Have you even eaten yet?" Hard to tell. In spite of her pregnancy not much more than seven weeks ago, she was slender. Maybe too slender this soon after having given birth.

"I ate," she said indignantly, but her eyes didn't quite meet his.

"What did you eat?"

She got a stubborn tilt to her mouth, and suddenly he was remembering what it was like to cross-examine someone who didn't want him to look too closely at her comings and goings. A sharp sense of unease came over him.

"All right, you ate," he agreed. "I haven't."

A look of distress darkened her pretty brown eyes. "Oh, no, Seth. I'm keeping you from your dinner."

Okay, he had lied a little. He had eaten, just not in the past hour. But he wasn't the one he was worried about.

"Look," he said, "my place is about as clean as it's going to get after the way you've been attacking it, and I haven't restocked my pantry so there's no point in your coming over to cook me a meal. Why don't you go back inside, I'll hike two blocks over to the deli and bring back something." He knew she was going to object, so he rushed on. "You won't mind if I eat here, will you?"

"Oh," she said, blinking. "No. No, of course not. You're sure about this, Seth?"

He lifted a shoulder. "It's just food, Molly. No big deal, right?"

"No, it's not." But her eyes were like dessert plates. Because it was a big deal. For her, a woman with secrets and for him, a man who courted solitude out of necessity. Sharing a meal with another person broke some universal law for people like her and him.

But he'd be damned if he was going to see her running herself into the ground because of some silly perceived debt she owed him.

Surely he could eat one meal with her without doing anything too idiotic or dangerous.

It struck him as he left to retrieve the food that this was the first time in years that he was doing something remotely ordinary. Having a meal with another human being, and not just any human being, either. A beautiful haunted woman with skin like rich cream, lips like wild berries and curves that made him ache whenever he thought of her.

How ordinary was that?

"It's just a meal, McCabe," he repeated when he was already a block away from her place. "So keep your mind and your hands off her curves. Touching her would be a sin."

But it wasn't as if he hadn't sinned before, was it?

Molly put Ruthie into her baby swing and set about tidying her apartment. Not that there was very much out of place, but after all, they were having company for dinner.

She tried not to think too hard about the fact that it

was Seth who was coming over, and she would be, for all intents and purposes, alone with him.

"Sorry, but you don't look much like a chaperone, sweetie," she told her child.

Ruthie gave an indignant crow, kicking her feet where they hung down.

"Right, like you're really going to tell Mom to knock it off if I start salivating over the man. You smile at him every time you look at him. You're just as bad as every other woman in the world."

Ruthie Ann wrinkled her nose and laughed, obviously in complete agreement.

"No flirting," she warned her daughter. "You and I upset him. He's just trying to be nice. Our only job is to be polite and not cause him any more trouble than we already have."

Ruthie didn't say a word. Clearly she hadn't made up her mind whether she wanted to go along with Molly's plan or not. Too late, anyway. The doorbell was ringing.

Molly rushed for the door and, assuming it was Seth, she almost threw it open, but just at the critical moment, she caught herself. What if it wasn't Seth?

Approaching the viewer, her heart pounded thunderously. This was a lot like looking under the bed to see if the boogeyman was there. Scary, because other than her landlord, whom she hadn't seen that much of, given her short stay, no one had ever rung her doorbell.

It was most likely Seth on the other side, but if not... Kevin *was* still out there somewhere. Fear clawed at her.

Gathering her courage, she peeked and saw Seth standing there tall and fierce, every scarred inch of him. She pulled open the door, relief flooding her. It was all she could do to keep from launching herself into his arms. And if she did that?

He would be gone, or he would never let her in his apartment ever again. She didn't know much about Seth, but she was pretty darn sure he didn't want some crazy overemotional, overly lusty woman on his hands.

She took a deep breath and offered up a simple smile.

"Come in," she managed to say, and she hoped it didn't sound as if she were inviting him into her bed. "Ruthie and I were just having a deeply philosophical conversation about the merits of a good—" she breathed in deeply "—corned-beef sandwich."

"Heavy topic," he agreed, and surprised her by smiling at her. Second time today. Something good must have happened. She was happy that finally there was something in his world to make him happy and so she returned the gesture. Not that she could help it. Just the way his upturned lips transformed his face made it imperative that a woman either give the man a simple smile or jump him and rip his clothes off.

And what in heck was wrong with her today? Must be the fact that it had been almost two months since she had given birth to Ruthie and with all the work she had been doing, her body was returning to normal.

"Ruthie and I like to have at least one serious conversation a day. It makes up for all the…um, bodily fluids discussions a mom ends up having with her child otherwise. But I guess you wouldn't know about that."

"I guess not," he agreed. "Babies are a bit outside my realm."

For a second she couldn't help wondering just what his realm was. She knew he worked in the middle of the night. Did that involve manual labor? Women? She knew so little of him.

Was she wrong to let him in? She closed her eyes for a second and remembered what she could of that ride to the hospital, the way he had taken care of everything.

"Let's eat," she said, and directed him to her kitchen table.

He walked past her, and once again she was reminded of how tall he was, how broad his shoulders. She wished she could touch—just once—the dark swish of his hair. And when she breathed in, she smelled the clean saddle-soap scent of him. He always smelled so clean.

Except that first time, she remembered. How could she remember that when so much was a blur?

She didn't know. Perhaps she was wrong, but there had been something very different about Seth that night. He dressed in black all the time. Simple things, but neat and clean. That night he had worn something else. She didn't know what it was, but his scent and his look had been different.

Once again, she was reminded of how much a man could fool a woman. She, more than other women, knew that a man could change and turn on her and threaten all the things most dear to her.

She glanced up at Seth.

And found him staring at her.

After her most recent thoughts, she should have been scared out of her wits.

Instead, she felt an indefinable urge to slip her hand beneath his shirt and see how his skin felt.

"Ready?" he asked, reaching for the plates she had left on the table.

She almost jumped, even though she understood what he was asking. It had everything to do with food and not a thing to do with the wanton desire coursing through her.

"I—I think so." But she wasn't really ready for a thing. Confusion filled her soul.

"Molly, I'm sorry. I'm making you nervous."

"No, it's all right."

"What is? The fact that I keep wanting to touch you?"

"You do?" She choked the words out.

"I do, but you don't have to worry. I'm controlling myself. I won't lay a hand on you. It wouldn't be right…for either of us."

He took a step back. She realized that she had been holding her breath, that she was a bit…disappointed, frustrated, anguished…and incredibly grateful for his restraint.

"Thank you," she said weakly. "You're right. No matter how much we both want it, we shouldn't touch."

After all, she was a woman on the run and she could have no future, at least not an ordinary one, because she couldn't admit to her past.

She already had enough trouble in her life with Kevin. She'd be crazy to invite more trouble, by falling into bed with Seth. But suddenly crazy looked very good...

Progress was slow, and he didn't like slow, Kevin thought, but in the end it wouldn't matter. He would still get what he wanted, even if it took longer than he liked.

He had clippings from old movie magazines, celebrity rags and tabloids that were yellowed but still readable after twenty years. And Molly had a face...such a face...people remembered her.

At least people who were over a certain age remembered her.

"We don't do the milk-carton stuff," one local dairy had told him. "Too depressing for people, and besides, there are so many. It gets bewildering. We've already got the advertising for our cartons booked for the next few months. But yeah, now that you mention it, I do remember that kid. I used to watch her all the time. Are you telling me she's the one missing? She must be at least twentysomething by now." The man looked suspicious.

"Twenty-four, but she's not the one I'm worried about, although yes, I am looking for her. The truth is that she's mentally unstable and has been for a while,"

Kevin told him. "She ran away, and she took my little girl with her. I'm afraid she's going to hurt the baby. Are you sure you can't help me?"

The man looked at the picture. "Well, she was a celebrity, a kid star. That might prove to be a big seller, even if it is a bit depressing to be reading that kind of stuff over your morning cereal."

"She's got a distinctive face. People would want to look out for her, to become a part of history."

The man rubbed his chin. "All right, the dairy's been having a few problems lately. Sales are down. So… maybe we could run the picture for a couple of weeks."

And so it had gone. Local newspapers, people on the street, small companies. Little by little, he was building the web. His little brown-haired beauty was going to get caught in it very soon, and then…?

"Then we won't need any other people, baby, because what's happening after that is just between you and me and is nobody else's business."

He smiled. It had been a reasonably good day and the days that followed promised to be even better.

Chapter 11

Molly was just getting ready to let Seth out of her apartment when someone rapped on the door.

Immediately she felt the blood drain from her face, her legs turned to jelly, her breathing went shallow. It couldn't be a friend this time. Seth was here. Ada didn't even know where she lived.

Bile rose in her throat. She looked at the door as if it were the devil incarnate. What should she do?

Run, run, run, her heart told her.

"Molly?" Seth's voice was worried. "Stay right here. Better yet, go into the other room. I'll get that." He started toward the door.

Her teeth were nearly chattering, but when Molly

saw Seth moving toward her door, intent on handling the situation, she was able at last to breathe in, to think.

Kevin Rickman was a man who would stop at nothing to get what he wanted. Did that include getting rid of anyone who stood in his way? If that was him and Seth tried to protect her, he wouldn't know who Kevin was. And if Kevin was wearing his uniform, Seth would be at a real disadvantage. He might be walking into danger for her sake.

Swiftly she scooted around Seth. "I'm sorry. I was just startled for a moment," she said, her voice weak but functioning. "I'll get that."

He stared at her, his dark eyes telling her he was aware of her discomfort. "Are you expecting someone?"

Should she lie? No, she had a feeling Seth was pretty good at seeing through lies. Judging by what she'd told him at the hospital and by the fact that her days were pretty much booked full with work and her activities at Ada's, he would know she hadn't been socializing.

"It might be important," she said, evading the question. And the truth was that she had to make sure it wasn't Kevin. If it was, she would have to run far and fast.

The person outside pounded on the door again.

"It might be trouble," Seth said, countering her last statement.

How right he was. "If it looks like trouble, I won't open the door."

"And you would know what trouble looks like?"

She thought of Kevin's sneering grin when he told

her of his plans for her child. "Oh, yes, I have a pretty good idea."

His expression told her that he didn't believe her.

"Seth," Molly said, her voice cracking with strain. "I have to live alone. I have to make my way and deal with my problems." She wouldn't take that back. Clearly he knew that she had a past and that it wasn't totally ordinary. Otherwise she wouldn't have ended up on the pavement going into labor alone. "You can't always be here to protect me. I have to do it myself. So I'm going to check the door. I would appreciate it if you would let me know if I make any serious mistakes. I'm all Ruthie has. Do you see how it is?"

"I do see." Grudgingly he stepped back and let her head for the door.

Every step she took, her feet felt as if cement were weighing them down. Who *was* at her door?

Her heart thudding hard, Molly peered through the viewfinder. A young boy stood waiting, shifting from foot to foot. He looked nearly as uncomfortable as she felt.

Without hesitation, she pulled back the door. "Yes, may I help you?"

"I'm selling candy to help raise money for my team's new baseball uniforms. Would you like to buy a box?" His voice came out squeaky, and he looked from side to side as if he would rather be doing anything else in the world.

Molly's heart went out to him. She thought of the

meager amount of money in her wallet. When she had fled her old home, she had taken as much money as she could out of her account, but between her rent, the food bills and the needs of a new baby, her funds were slipping. The bakery didn't pay all that much, and she didn't dare try to touch her accounts now. Still, she nodded and turned to go get her wallet.

Seth stopped her with a touch. He gave her a bill, which she pressed into the boy's hand, and the boy handed over a box of chocolates. "Thank you," the boy said. He started to go.

Seth cleared his throat. "Does your mother know you're going door-to-door?" and the boy's frightened expression told even the most naive listener that he was about to lie.

"Here," Seth said, and handed the boy several large bills.

The boy blinked. He stammered his thanks and turned over the remains of his box of supplies. "Don't let me catch you doing this again," Seth said.

"No sir," and the boy quickly lit out for the street.

After he had gone and Molly had closed the door, she smiled up at Seth. "That was wonderful of you," she said.

He scowled. "It was completely stupid. You'll have every kid in the neighborhood showing up from here on out."

He was probably right. The thought should have panicked her, and in some ways it did, but in another better way, she felt warm and right inside. She had been hiding like a mouse for weeks, living a life that had little semblance to an ordinary human's reality. Here in this moment, Seth and a kid selling candy had brought a small touch of reality, a bit of light into her life. How ironic that that light should come from a man who courted the darkness and was obviously unhappy with this night's work.

"It was stupid," he said again, ignoring the fact that he had ensured a young boy's safety. "The last thing you need is more people ringing your doorbell. Do me a favor?"

"What?"

"Don't open your door anymore to anyone you don't absolutely know."

"I won't," she promised as he left her apartment, stepped out into the night and walked away. But what she didn't tell him was that the person she feared most was someone she did know all too well. She supposed he was also right about the boy. His actions might bring more kids to her door.

It also had a second effect. She couldn't help wanting to know more about a man who absolutely insisted he didn't want to get involved and yet dropped a big chunk of change for candy he hadn't even taken with him.

Seth McCabe obviously had demons that haunted him; yet he couldn't keep himself from helping those he seemed to think needed saving.

She wanted to know why. Who was Seth, anyway, and why was he helping her?

It was a question Seth was asking himself the very next day as he sat in his room, waiting for Molly to finish doing whatever she was doing out in his kitchen. He had taken the easy way out again today. He'd done it because, when that doorbell had rung yesterday and she had frozen with fear, he had barely been able to stop himself from folding his arms around her, from telling her that he would risk everything to keep her from whatever was scaring her.

That was even more stupid than the stunt he had pulled with that kid. What on earth had he been thinking?

But he knew the answer to that.

"Shannon." He mouthed the word. When Shannon had been in her early teens, she and a friend had hatched up a scheme to buy cosmetics and sell them door-to-door. She admitted later that she was trying to raise enough money to allow her to run away from her overly protective, overly strict brother.

It had almost torn him in two, but it had been nothing compared to his fears when he caught her at it. She'd been marching up to the door of an older man who had been looking at her with all too much interest lately. Seth's blood had turned to ice. Consequently he had practically snapped his baby sister's head off, berating her endlessly…eventually, driving her away. At almost eighteen, unwilling to let him smother her with restrictions, she had gone. In the end, she had gotten her heart and soul mangled, anyway.

When he'd seen that kid yesterday, his mind had gone blank. As if he could make the past right, live it over again, he had taken a different tack this time, bought out the kid's candy in an attempt to achieve what he'd wanted to achieve with Shannon, to save that scruffy boy from his sister's fate.

Heck, that was dumb. The kid probably wouldn't ever consider running away from home the way his sister had. He was probably a kiddie con who knew far more about protecting himself on the street than an adult like Molly did. And now, she, who went dead-white at the sound of a doorbell ringing, might have to listen to it ring time and time again.

"Damn it, McCabe, you fool!" he said.

"Seth?" Molly's voice came from beyond the door, sweet and low. "Are you…are you all right?"

Just the sound of her voice licked his senses, made him hot. He thought of the curve of her lips, the sweet swell of her breasts, how her fingers felt like butterflies dancing against his skin, making him crazy to touch her. Was he all right? No, not at all. He was going slowly insane, hiding from a woman who didn't have the power of a mouse in her muscles but who could bring him to his knees wanting what he could never allow himself.

"Just dropped something," he muttered. And then, because he felt like a jerk hiding from her, he opened the door. As if he didn't have a drop of self-control, he emerged into the room.

"You almost done?" he asked gruffly, forcing himself to frown at her.

She ignored his attitude and smiled at him, indicating the table where she had laid a feast complete with flowers.

"Molly, your hard-earned money," he couldn't help admonishing. "Don't waste it on me."

"Oh." She blushed, and he hated himself for making her self-conscious. "Mr. Alex lets me take them from the display window at the end of the day. They're nothing special."

His throat grew tight. She had so little, she worked so hard and lived with whatever it was that had left her alone in the world.

"They're lovely," he said, and he couldn't help reaching out and sliding his finger down her cheek even though one touch only made him long for more. "I'm a bit rusty with thank-yous. Don't mind me. I'm a beast," he said, his voice rough edged. *I'm a reporter when you told me you hated them,* he thought. *And I can't even tell you the truth.*

"A beast who saved us," she said solemnly, swallowing hard at his touch. "Right, Ruthie?"

The cherub on the floor sucked her fist, her eyes bright and happy, her legs kicking. Seth prayed for a world where kids like Ruthie would never know pain, but looking at Molly and searching his own soul, he knew that the odds were against her.

"Any man who could walk past that one and not help her has no right to call himself a man," he said.

Molly blinked. She probably knew that any help he gave her he did so reluctantly.

"You'd better be on your way," he said quietly. "It'll be dark soon."

She nodded. "You work very late, don't you?"

"I've got some time yet," he answered simply. What would she think if she knew that he reported on people who didn't know that the man in their midst was the one writing about them? He told other people's stories while jealously guarding his own privacy. "It's you who needs to be in before dark falls." He didn't offer more.

"Sorry," she said. "I didn't mean to pry. I don't like people who butt into other people's business."

"You have a right to ask questions. The answer is, yes, I work very late. And you get up very early."

She grinned. "Okay, I'm going. You don't have to kick me down the stairs."

"A relief," he said with a small smile, and she chuckled.

"Come on, Ruthie Ann. Seth is feeling overwhelmed with all our femaleness. I think it was the flowers."

Ruthie said something unintelligible, which might have been agreement. She waited patiently and round eyed as her mother bundled her into her coat.

"You're going to need something bigger to carry her in soon. A stroller or something," he said, but at the panicked look on her face, he realized that she might not be able to afford such an item.

"I like holding her," she said.

"Well, there you have it. No stroller needed," he agreed, sorry he had made her uncomfortable even for a second.

And then he listened to the sounds of Molly's muffled footsteps on the carpeting as she made her way down the stairs. Ada wasn't in, having gone to a movie with the girls, and so Molly moved out onto the street.

He stepped to the nearest window and watched her. As he did, he saw two men trailing her. They didn't appear to be together, but no matter. They definitely appeared to be interested in her movements, and she was holding a baby. How on earth would she be able to run?

Seth tore down the stairs and out onto the street. He didn't bother trying to be quiet.

One man peeled off, the clean-cut guy heading in the opposite direction. Seth let him go, because the other one was still looking Molly's way.

She had turned the corner, and when the scumbag followed suit, Seth slipped up behind him, tucked his arm around the guy's throat and tugged hard. The guy kicked back with an *oof* and there was a clatter as Seth skidded on the pavement and banged into a street sign.

Molly must have heard the noise, because she picked up her pace and rounded another corner.

Good girl, he wanted to tell her, but at the moment, getting some information from the dirtbag was the best he could do.

He leaned slightly, throwing the guy off balance, then shoved back the other way, slamming him against a nearby brick wall and pinioning him there.

Seth scowled, knowing that his scars could be plenty scary given the right expression and the right circumstances.

"You looking for something, punk?" he asked softly.

The guy shifted his eyes as if looking for an out. He was ready to run.

"I wouldn't try. I carry a knife at all times." Which was only part of the truth. He carried two knives.

"I wasn't doin' nothin'," the guy whined, and Seth saw that he wasn't much more than a kid.

"You were following that woman, weren't you?"

"Who says?"

Seth gave him another shove into the wall. "Don't be stupid. There's nobody on this street except you and me. I could slit you from neck to knees and leave you here. Who would know or care?"

And the guy started sweating. He struggled in Seth's grasp. "I wasn't gonna hurt her," he squealed. "Honest. All I wanted was her purse."

From the wild, frightened look in the man's eyes, Seth could tell that he, most likely, wasn't lying. "Yeah, well you got me instead."

"Really, I wouldn't have hurt her."

"Scaring her wasn't a good idea, either."

"I know, I know. What are you going to do with me?"

Seth considered that. If he turned the guy in, they'd let him out on the street in no time, since there was no real proof that he had evil intent. But letting the guy go this way just wasn't an option.

"I'll tell you what," Seth said slowly, evenly. "I'm not even going to nick you today. But—" he patted around the guy until he found a slew of credit cards and ID's "—which are you, Brendan Lanhart or George Mosella?"

The guy gave a snort. "Neither. The guys call me Hot Hands, because I'm such a good pickpocket."

Little twit. By the way he said the nickname with such pride, Seth could tell he was telling the truth.

"Well, Hot Hands, I even hear a whisper that you went near the lady there again, I'll pay a private visit to you, and your hands won't be so hot from here on out. You follow?"

The kid had the guts or stupidity to smile. "How do I know you even got a knife?"

Seth could have shown him, but he had no intention of letting Hot Hands call the shots. Instead, Seth just gave an evil smile. "You see this scar?" He indicated the longest one on his face.

"Yeah?"

"It's a nick compared to what I'll give you. If you'd like, I can demonstrate right now. Just let me get the right tool." He set the kid back on the ground. Immediately, the guy started to back away.

Seth laughed, just for effect. "Oh, and Hot Hands?"

"What?"

"You know Louie, who sits on the corner next to Ralph's Liquors?"

"What about him?"

"He'll tell me if you do something stupid."

That was enough to get rid of the guy's smirk. Louie had lost his sight years ago in a fight, but he listened to everything on the streets. He knew almost everything. If someone got mugged, Louie could tell you and he could most likely tell you who did it and maybe even where to find him.

"Louie and I go way back."

The kid swore and scurried away. "I didn't even touch her," he called back.

"See that you don't."

When the guy had gone, Seth slumped against the wall. The thought of Hot Hands approaching Molly, scaring her, assaulting her in any way, made him weak. He wanted to roar, to scream, to bundle her up in cotton and protect her.

But it had never worked that way in his lifetime, and Molly wanted and needed more than someone to protect her. She needed to have the skills to do it herself.

He needed to make sure that she had those skills.

Setting out at a trot, Seth headed toward her house. The falling darkness closed around him, which was a relief of some sort, but not enough. Not nearly enough.

She had been scared when she had turned that corner. Heaven help that whelp he had just set free if he had done her any permanent damage.

Seth ran up to her apartment building, and what he saw there sent him into a rage. Her side window was open two inches.

He raced inside and down the hall. Banging on the door, he waited.

No answer.

"Damn it all to hell, McCabe," he said to himself. "What do you expect? You beat on her door like a madman and expect her to open to you?"

"Molly?" he called, banging on the door again, hoping that his voice alone would be enough to reassure her that some stranger wasn't trying to get to her.

And then the door opened.

She stood there, eyes wide and scared, pretty face pale. She was safe.

And he was unable to find an outlet for all that had passed in the last few minutes.

"Do you have no sense of self-preservation?" he roared, pointing to her window. "Don't you know this isn't the country? You can't just leave your windows open at night. At least you can't if you're a woman living on the first floor and you live alone. Don't you know that?"

He saw her try to swallow. She passed one hand over her mouth.

Okay, damn it, he was the lowest heel on earth. She was scared. He was scaring her even more.

"I...someone tried to follow me. I lost him and I came home, but I couldn't breathe. I needed air. I was sitting by the window, prepared to close it in just a second."

She had been scared, so scared she needed air, and now some jerk was standing here yelling at her, berating her, angry. But the anger was at himself, he knew, because he was so wrong for her and yet he couldn't stay away from her. His life was secret, with danger built right in, and not only that, but he couldn't do the caring thing again. He just couldn't. He had lost so much in spite of all of his efforts. His parents, his sister. Nothing he had done had worked. Losing someone you cared about could make you crazy. Heck, maybe he was crazy right now. He should leave her alone.

Yet still he wanted her, even knowing that would be all wrong for Molly. She was alone, vulnerable and not a woman a man could touch with no thought for tomorrow.

"I'm sorry," he said, somehow managing to make his voice softer. "You just—you have to be more careful."

"I know. I know." Her tone was less contrite than soothing. He could see what she was doing. She was trying to comfort *him* when she was the one who had nearly been attacked, when she was the one who was being yelled at. "Don't worry. I will be careful," she said even more soothingly. And she took a step closer.

It was too much, all of this. Seth reached out. He snaked one arm around her and pulled her even closer and then he leaned down and tasted her lips. At last. He plundered her mouth, he took without asking, just like the rat he was.

He angled his head and kissed her solidly, thoroughly and then he pulled back. He gazed at her, looked into those luminous dark and trusting eyes.

Her lips trembled and so he kissed them again. More softly this time.

She rose up on her toes, placed one hand lightly on his chest and returned his kiss. So soft, so tentative. He thought his heart might stop beating right then and there.

But then his heartbeat returned and so did his sanity.

He stepped back. But he didn't apologize. He had wanted to touch her, and now he had. This would be the end of it.

At least now he knew how hot the fire burned.

Far too hot. He was the worst thing in the world for her.

"Tomorrow I start teaching you how to defend yourself. When we're done, we're done," he said. "And then you won't have to worry anymore."

He closed her window and then he left her there, making sure her door locked tight behind him.

She was safe now. From the world.

And from him.

Chapter 12

Molly lifted the curtain at her window and watched Seth fade away into the ever-increasing shadows. She touched her lips and wished she could hold on to the sensation of Seth's mouth against hers.

But already it was disappearing, like the man himself.

"It's probably for the best," she whispered. After all, she didn't really know anything about him, except that he had done her several kindnesses and he worried about a young boy risking his safety by going door-to-door. Oh, yes, she also knew that a crotchety old woman thought he made the sun come up every morning, even if he seemed to favor the dark hours of the night.

And she knew one thing more. He had wanted to kiss her, but he hadn't been happy when he had done so.

His lips had been rough at first. She hadn't cared, she had wanted him so much. But when she'd looked up at him, his eyes had been angry and she was sure that the anger hadn't been directed at her. Seth had told her that he would teach her defensive measures and then he would be gone.

He might desire her, but he didn't want to be around her anymore. Not that he ever had. Her inability to protect herself and Ruthie was what had sent him back to her time and time again.

And now he wanted out for good.

Oh, hell. Why did that hurt? Shouldn't she just be happy that Seth was willing to teach her what she needed to know?

"Is it possible that we can stay hidden from Kevin forever?" She shivered, wrapping her arms tightly around herself. Who knew? But she knew this much. Kevin had gone to great lengths to snare her in the first place. She was pretty sure that he had always planned on impregnating her, too, because he had smiled when he'd told her that the condom he'd used must have been faulty. And not much later he had admitted that he wanted their baby to be another child star and was already trying to set up jobs.

That was when she had gotten scared, when she realized that he had chosen her because of who she had once been rather than because of who she was now. It was when he had gotten mean, or at least when he finally let it show.

Getting up the nerve to run had taken a while, but during that time she had seen how ruthless he really was.

What if he found out how much Seth had helped her? For Seth's sake, she should stay away from him.

"I will, once he teaches me what I need to know to keep Ruthie safe," she promised herself.

She stroked her fingertips over her lips. Surely she could control her need to touch Seth until then.

Molly stared out into the gathering gloom and wondered where he was and what he was doing right now. What did he do with his nights?

Seth found a good corner with a brick wall at his back, plenty of shadows to hide him and a streetlight that revealed much of the street before him. He prepared to settle down for a night of watching.

He needed this, needed to be productive. Mostly he needed to forget that he had kissed Molly and what it had felt like. A muscle in his jaw jerked at the thought.

He shifted and slouched so that his coat came up around his ears. Staying still kept people from noticing you too much. It kept you alive. He was having a hell of a time keeping still tonight, though. Molly's taste was on his tongue, sweet and warm, making him want to dip back in for another sip.

Seth shifted again.

The man closest to him grunted. "That you, Lightning?"

Damn, now he had done it.

Seth looked up. "Shuffle?"

"Heard you mixed it up with a kid called Hot Hands today."

Uh-oh. "I'm surprised anyone noticed."

"They didn't. Kid's been talking to anyone who'll listen. His description sounded like you. He wants you cut."

"Yeah? So who's gonna try?"

Shuffle chuckled, then coughed, wheezing loudly with the cold. "Probably nobody. Don't know the kid, but I heard he's a snot-nosed, irritating runt. Why'd you tangle?"

Seth knew better than to hesitate. "I don't like anybody who preys on women."

The other man looked his way, but Seth knew he couldn't see too much. "Who does?" he said. "He hurt her?"

"No."

"Good. I'll let you know if I hear he's made any connections."

"Thanks."

And then things got quiet. Shuffle was already starting to snore when a truck pulled up and a small group of people climbed out and started passing soup and bread around. It was a bitter night, and Seth knew how welcome the food was to these men.

"You're an angel," Rip said, sketching an elegant bow to the middle-aged woman who handed him his soup and a spoon. In spite of his tattered appearance there was still a thread of dignity to the man.

"You'd be better off at the shelters," she said.

"Maybe, but someone stole my coat the last time. Not everyone who goes there is just looking for food."

"I suppose," she said, but she still didn't sound happy.

"But thank you, my dear," Rip said again. "It's good of you to come out in the cold to see to us."

The man with her passed Rip a small loaf of bread. "We read today's 'Mean Streets' column. Nick Dawson said that some of the men here were too embarrassed to ask for help. We thought if we simply offered it might be less awful. Everybody needs a hand now and then."

"That Nick, he's somethin', ain't he?" Shuffle, who had awakened, asked. "I read one of those columns where he talked about what it was like to sleep on the ground, not knowing if someone was going to rob you or slit your throat before morning came. It was spooky, like he really understood. Wonder how he made it so real."

"He probably does those interviews," Snap told him.

"Not us. Nobody ever interviewed us," Shuffle said. "How'd you find us?" he asked the man and woman.

The man shrugged. "Just headed into the city and drove around."

"Brave man," Don't Look told him.

"Dawson must be brave, too. Takes guts to keep writing about people like us when he could be interviewing the rich and famous."

A chuckle sounded from one of the men. He hoisted his bowl of soup. "To the kind folks here and to Nick Dawson," he said. "If I ever find out who he is, I'll shake his hand."

Not possible. If anyone found out who Nick Dawson really was, Seth thought, no one here would ever feel comfortable around him again. He would be a reporter, not one of them. And reporters could only interview and speculate. They couldn't live with their subjects in the hopes of shedding some light and making their world a better, safer place. His column would be over and any good he had done would be finished.

Shannon had lived on the streets, and now Molly traversed them with her child.

He held back his groan. He definitely needed to be more careful than he had been lately. That business with Hot Hands had been pretty stupid. No one here ever saw him in his other life. If they did, they would know he wasn't one of them.

"But if he ever goes near her again," he whispered to himself later once dawn had streaked in, and the city workers were shooing people from their roosts, "he'll live to regret it, and to hell with my cover."

He would have to train Molly well. The thought of being with her that way made him dizzy with need.

"Can it, McCabe," he told himself. "Think of it as just another job." This time, if he did things right, no one would get hurt. And when he was done, she could carry on with her life without him.

The thought was like a new knife nick, to the heart this time, but that was just too damn bad.

"So let's jump off the cliff and get started," he said.

"You sure Ada doesn't mind watching Ruthie?" Molly asked for the fourth time as she and Seth left Ada's apartment and moved onto the darkening street.

Seth took her arm. "You asked her, didn't you? She said she was thrilled."

"Maybe she was just being nice."

Seth stopped in his tracks. "Ada? You're kidding, right?"

Molly poked him in the chest. "Ada is a very nice woman."

"Ada is the best," Seth agreed, "but she never says things just to be nice. More than anyone I know, Ada is completely, unfailingly honest. It's one of the best things about her. She doesn't lie to make people feel good."

Molly wondered what kinds of things Ada had said to Seth to make him surmise that, but it wasn't the kind of thing she had any business asking.

"Okay, I'm good with this, then. What do I need to know? Where do we start? Are you going to teach me how to use a knife?"

Seth had been leading her down the street, but at that last suggestion, he turned and glared at her. "Hell, no."

"Don't I need to be able to defend myself?"

"If you have a knife, it can be taken from you and used against you."

She stared at him, wanting to ask him how he'd gotten those scars. The thought of someone attacking him made her furious.

"It wasn't my own knife," he said, as if he had read her mind.

"Still…it must have been…awful…painful."

"Don't think about it." He nudged her around a hole in the sidewalk. "You don't have to, because it won't happen to you." His jaw was tight, his eyes such dark pools of anger and determination that she almost believed he could protect her by sheer will. Not true, of course. *She* had to learn the ropes.

"So what are you going to teach me?" she asked, and this time his expression softened. For a moment she could barely keep herself from leaning into him, from asking him to teach her what it felt like to touch all of him, to make love with him. She ached to feel his naked skin against hers, and for a woman in her situation, that was so wrong.

He reached out and cupped her jaw. "Don't worry. We'll keep you safe. Let's start with the basics—how to know when someone is following you and how to discourage them from doing so."

And so they walked. He showed her how to always appear alert, to look at people in a way that let them know she was aware of their every move, and no, she wasn't interested in knowing them.

When a news truck stopped in traffic almost right next to them, Molly lurched and ended up bumping into Seth. He swung her down a side street. "It's all right," he said. "They're not interested in us." He studied her closely. She felt her cheeks flush, but didn't even try to explain.

And he didn't ask. Instead, he taught her to watch for movements in the shadows, to listen for the slightest tap of a shoe on pavement, the click of a car door, the metallic *whoosh* of a van door sliding open. He made her pretend he was a guy considering accosting her. She passed every test, even when he took her on the subway and devised role-playing games. That one had her worried in more ways than one. A police officer stared at Seth. For a minute, she thought the officer was going to approach Seth. Fear rushed in. She had to remind herself that not every policeman was like Kevin.

But then Seth spoke to her. It became obvious that he was with her, and the officer moved away.

"Don't take risks like that," she whispered. "You might have been arrested."

"I was testing you. You should have gotten the officer's attention."

"Oh."

"Next time…" he instructed her.

"Next time," she agreed, but she knew that the next time she would still be more afraid of the officer than she was of Seth. It didn't make any sense, and she promised herself to do the right thing if it ever became necessary. But it wouldn't be easy. Kevin was like a silent threat everywhere she went, and the uniform was a part of that.

They moved back onto the street and Seth continued to put Molly through her paces. The last time, he came up behind her, silently in an area where there wasn't an easy escape, so she turned and stared at him, her chin lifted high, her eyes never leaving him. She grabbed her key ring hanging from the edge of her purse and held out the pepper spray that was attached to it. She even opened her mouth to scream *Fire*.

Seth walked toward her, applauding. "You are magnificent," he told her. "Escape if you can, and if that's just not possible, let the jerk know that you know his game and that you see his face. In the future, carry an umbrella, something you can use at a distance. It's better than keys, which you have to be in close to use. But you're doing just fine. You've got the attitude. You're telling him that you won't be an easy target, because you know that's what he's looking for. Make as much noise as you can. Chances are good that he's just a coward looking for an opportunity. Don't give him one, and he might run off looking for easier prey."

That unsettled her a bit. "I don't want someone else getting hurt."

"You can't save everyone, Molly," he said, and his voice seemed rougher than usual. "Ruthie and yourself, that's all I want you to think about. Pray that the other people know how to keep themselves out of harm's way, too. If you don't think that way, your daughter might be the one to suffer. You have to keep her safe, and keep yourself safe for her."

She fiddled with her purse. "I know that."

He moved closer and touched her cheek. "I'm sorry," he said, softly. "So sorry it has to be this way."

That was almost her undoing. He was close, his fingers warm on her skin. If she leaned, she could breathe him in.

Molly stepped back. "Do I pass?"

"Oh, yeah," he told her. "Flying colors and all that. For tonight."

Her eyes widened. "Tonight?"

"The trick is to keep people at a distance, but if that's not possible, then you need to know some basic tricks about how to get away," he told her. "Look at me, Molly."

She stared up into his eyes, which were dark with intent, and her breath caught in her throat. The scars weren't even there in her mind. All she saw was Seth, trying to help her.

Molly swallowed hard. "Yes?"

"I want to make very sure you're safe. I'm hoping with everything I am that you never, ever need to know how to defend yourself, but if you do, I need to know that you can get away without so much as a bruise." His voice was gruff. He had moved nearer. She breathed him in.

"You're so..." *Wonderful,* she wanted to say, but she was afraid. He hadn't wanted this. Fate had dumped her on him, and she had dragged him in deeper.

"You're very good to us," she said instead. "Ruthie

and I are lucky that you were the one who found us that night."

He turned his head to the side, looking away. "I'm just a man, and a very fallible one, Molly. Don't make me more, and don't think I'm any kind of saint. I've already let you know that I want you."

"But you won't take me."

He laughed. "Maybe I *am* a saint."

"Ah, you're laughing, but don't ask me to think less of you than I do," she said. "I get to decide what I think of you."

He tilted his head in acquiescence, and the night sky shone behind him. She realized that they had made it all the way to the lake. Adler Planetarium and the Shedd Aquarium lay on their left on a patch of land that jutted into the lake, the winter-deserted Burnham Harbor on their right. The moonlight cast its beams into the water.

"This is so lovely," she said. "I never realized that a city could look so beautiful. Standing here tonight, it's hard to remember that there are darker parts of the same city."

"I wish you never had to remember that, but—"

She touched his sleeve. "Don't worry. You're a good teacher. Thanks to you," she said with a smile, "I know how to dissuade any wolves that might approach me."

But he didn't return her smile.

"I didn't mean you."

"Nevertheless," he said. "I do want you."

"Maybe I want you, too."

Seth sucked in an audible breath. "That definitely wouldn't be best for you."

He was right, even though it made her chest hurt. "It would be…incredibly unwise," she agreed. And not only for her. It might not be safe for him to get entangled with her. She couldn't let Kevin hurt Seth.

"We'd better get back," Seth said. He hailed a cab and took her home. On the way, they passed through a neighborhood where some women were standing on the street corner. At least one of them was very young, her heavily made-up eyes not hiding the look of despair on her face.

When Molly glanced at Seth, he was like a man made of granite.

"Seth?"

He shook himself and turned to her, a smile on his face. It was the phoniest smile she had ever seen, and it wasn't like him to do that. "We're almost there," he told her.

Obviously he wasn't going to explain what that look had been about, and she didn't have a right to pry.

So they made it back to Ada's, picked up Ruthie, and Seth walked Molly home. When she had unlocked her door and turned back to him, he wasn't looking at her but at her daughter. "Keep her safe, Molly. Do everything you can."

"You know I will."

"I know you'll try."

"No matter what happens, I won't let anyone find her."

He blinked at that, and she realized she had made a misstep, but it was too late to take the comment back, and she wasn't going to explain, no matter how many questions her comment had called up.

"I can't tell you my secrets," she whispered. "I just can't. But I want you to know that you're helping. I won't let your lessons go to waste. I'll be a tigress if I have to."

He looked down at her for a moment. "The world doesn't deserve women like you, Molly." Then, brushing her lips, he gently pushed her inside and closed the door behind her.

"Lock it tight," he said, and when she had, she heard the sound of his footsteps on the tile moving away from her door. It was a terrible, lonely thought. Since the moment she had met Seth, he had been moving away from her.

And it was her responsibility to move away, too.

Chapter 13

That night, before going to work, Seth couldn't keep himself from making a detour to an area of small neatly kept apartment buildings some distance from his own neighborhood.

Circling around the back, he rapped lightly on the basement apartment door. An elderly woman, the landlady he had met only a few times before, answered. She shook her head. "Mr. McCabe, isn't it? Shannon's brother. What are you doing here?"

Good question. He knew he was the last person his sister wanted to ever see again, but that young girl on the street…

Seth took a deep breath of cold, clarifying air. "Not much. I'm not looking for Shannon, Mrs. Kotchki. I sent her a check a few weeks ago. It came back. I just wanted to make sure everything was all right." It was a stupid reason. Shannon had returned more checks than he cared to remember.

Evidently the woman wasn't buying into his excuse for being here, either. She eyed him suspiciously. "She pays her bills. I don't spy on my tenants as long as they pay their bills and don't give me any trouble." The implication that he was giving her trouble was pretty darn clear. He supposed it *was* rather late for a business call.

"I know this much," the woman said. "Shannon doesn't like anybody nosing into her business."

Yeah, he knew that, too. She had screamed at him many times, telling him to leave her alone. He hadn't listened, and his perseverance had had long-reaching consequences. Seth pushed away the scaldingly terrifying memory of the endless months he had spent searching for Shannon when he had found the note telling him she had run away to San Francisco.

"So she's okay?"

"I don't know if she's eating her vegetables or washing behind her ears, Mr. McCabe. I just know that she doesn't make too much noise, she gets the rent check in on time and she doesn't tick me off."

It was obvious that he *did* tick her off.

"Look, Mr. McCabe, I know you found this place for your sister, but that was a while ago. She's an adult, twenty-two, if my memory serves me well, and it always does. She's the one I rent to, and she's been living here several years. It would be wrong to talk to you without asking her."

And if she asked Shannon, Shannon would tell her to bar the door against him from now on. The lady was right. No matter what the situation had once been, his sister was an adult now and one who didn't want anything to do with her brother. He really had no right to check up on her, and in fact was already feeling guilty for having tried to.

He was feeling guilty about a lot of things. Molly had secrets, too. Dangerous ones, he guessed. The urge to rush in and help was even stronger with her, and even more wrong.

He turned to leave.

"Mr. McCabe?"

Seth stopped and looked over his shoulder.

"She's extra careful about keeping her door locked, if that helps." Mrs. Kotchki tossed the crumbs his way, and then she closed and locked her own door.

Seth lurched into the night. Did it help to know that his once fun-loving sister was careful about locking her doors? That depended. It helped to know that she was safe, but it didn't tell him a thing about how she was dealing with her demons.

And that was what haunted him. The fact that he had driven her to run away and discover those demons in the first place was what sent him back into the street every night.

"So get on with it, McCabe. Go chase your own demons and leave her alone, and while you're giving orders, keep your mind far away from Molly tonight. That last column was a piece of crap. You've got to do better."

But he knew nothing would keep Molly from his thoughts. Which was just too damn bad, since he could never have her.

That night he was filled with anger. He got into a fight with a guy who tried to steal Rip's hat, and Seth ended up with a gash on his hand. Still, he drove the other guy off into the night. He wouldn't be coming back.

"Thank you, Lightning," Rip said, looking a little concerned.

Thank Molly, Seth wanted to say. Normally he didn't interfere with what went on in the street. He just lived it and reported it. But tonight he had been trying to ignore the desire for Molly that was starting to be far too big a piece of his life. He had needed action, and so Rip now had his hat back in tow.

And he had called attention to himself once again.

"Let's see here now what we've got to choose from," Ada said to her friends who were gathered in her apartment. "We've got *An Affair to Remember, Bringing Up Baby, From Here to Eternity* and *Buffy, the Vampire Slayer.* Which will it be?" She held out the tapes in her hands.

"You picked out some good ones, Ada. And I like Buffy."

"Yeah, but the movie doesn't star Sarah Michelle Gellar," Cecily pointed out.

"Still fun."

"I know, but...I'm really in a Kate Hepburn kind of mood. I love those strong heroines."

"They're all strong heroines," Ada pointed out.

"You don't like Kate?"

"What's not to like?"

"Exactly. So there."

The other women stared at Cecily, who had clearly made up all their minds.

"You dog," Ada said. "That was tricky. But cute." She set the other three tapes down and started toward the VCR.

"Wait, wait," Dora said. "I wanted to show you. Look what I've got. A new subscription to *Entertainment Weekly* and one to *People*. Now we can get all the dirt on everyone." She held up the brightly colored magazines.

"Dora," Ada said. "You know I'm not into gossip."

Dora raised her brows. "Then you don't even want to know what new movie Johnny Depp is making? That's not gossip."

Ada licked her lips. "I might be interested."

Fran giggled. "You're so transparent, Ada."

"I like to call it honest."

"Call it what you will. What do you think of these? I was down at my church rummage sale and look what I picked up. They were just sitting there in a dusty pile and nobody even wanted them." She held out a paper bag, tipped it near the floor and spilled out its contents. Out came old yellowed copies of magazines. The one on top had a picture of Sean Connery on it, looking about twenty years younger than he did today.

"Fran, you've hit gold," Cecily said. "Be careful. They might rip."

"And there's more where that came from. I only brought one bag. One day soon when we get some time we'll have a magazine-organizing party. We'll gorge on old gossip. I mean on entertainment news," she said, smiling at Ada.

"Exactly," Ada said. "News is good. Gossip is bad…unless it's about Johnny. Then, sometimes, it's okay. Now, are we going to watch this movie or not?"

"In a minute. Just let me pick my magazines up," Fran said. "Let's see. We've got an article on beach movies, one on Ava Gardner, one on child stars, here's one on Julie Andrews…" She looked at each magazine as she put it into the bag.

"Hold on, back up. Let me see that one," Ada said, her voice tense.

"Which one?"

"Which one? The one on Julie Andrews. You know how much I love *The Sound of Music*. Couldn't you just eat Christopher Plummer with a big old spoon?" She plopped down with the magazine and started poring through it. Fran put the others back in the bag.

"Let's watch the movie," she said. "I'll make popcorn."

In just a few minutes they had all settled down with a tray of diet cola, popcorn and pretzels, their attention glued to the screen as Katharine Hepburn put Cary Grant through his paces.

Kate had finally worked her magic and the women were basking in the glow of a good movie they had all seen far too many times to count when a tentative knock sounded on the door.

"If you're not Cary Grant, go away," Ada grumbled.

"I would, but I've got fresh, warm chocolate chip cookies, and if I don't bring them in now, they'll get cold." Molly's voice sounded through the doorway.

"Warm chocolate chip cookies? You've just replaced Cary on my list of people I have to see," Ada said, and she got to her feet and went to let Molly in.

Molly grinned and held out the plate. "Isn't Cary Grant…um…deceased?"

"Doesn't matter. He's alive on film and still breakin' hearts, girl, but forget about him. Let's talk about these cookies. You make these in Seth's oven?"

Molly blinked, and her breathing began to race. "Um, no. I was just up at Seth's apartment, but he was— that is, when I went inside, he was still asleep." She hoped she wasn't blushing. She didn't even want to think about the moment when she had realized that she wasn't alone in the apartment and that the door to Seth's bedroom was open.

She had tried to resist peeking in, but…

He was on the bed, his dark hair tousled, one bare

leg and most of his chest sticking out from beneath navy sheets. Her mouth had gone dry and she had nearly bumped into the door and knocked over a lamp scooting out quickly. Before she had made her escape, she had gotten a swift glimpse of the pictures just inside his door. There was the girl with the blond hair and sunny smile, and a family shot—a dark-haired man who looked like an older version of Seth, a petite blond woman, the girl at a younger age, and Seth. Seth had been smiling. He was the most gorgeous male Molly had ever seen.

She must have made a noise, because he had stirred in his sleep. The cover had shifted as heat poured through her. That reaction was all it had taken to send her out the door. She hoped he never knew that she had watched him like that, that she had wanted him so badly it was all she could do to keep from asking Ada to watch Ruthie so she could crawl into bed with Seth.

That would have made the ladies here blush. Or maybe not. Ada was eyeing her speculatively. The other women were studying their fingernails much too carefully.

"He didn't wake up," she blurted out.

Ada lifted a brow. "Hmm, a pity. That would have been something to see. I'll bet Seth sleeps in the buff." She looked at Molly as if she expected her to answer the question.

"The cookies are from the bakery," Molly said in a choked whisper as she attempted to shift the subject.

"Mr. Alex's bakery? That man makes pastries and cookies to die for. If he wasn't married, I would tie him up naked and make him bake for me day and night," Cecily said.

Mr. Alex was a short, rotund man with a perpetual smile. He was also Molly's employer. "That is something I don't even want to think about," she said, pretending to cover her ears.

When she reached up, Ruthie, who was in a carrier on Molly's back, let out a delighted squeal.

"Do not listen to them, sweetie," Molly told her daughter with a grin. "They will corrupt you. You're too young for fantasies, even ones about chocolate chip cookies."

Ruthie bucked and squealed again.

"Oh, she wants out of there. Can I hold her?" Dora asked, and soon the four women were clucking over the baby much more than they had over Cary Grant. So Molly was the only one who heard Seth's light tap on the door.

She peeked out and saw him. He had put on a shirt, but she could still envision what his naked chest had looked like. She hoped she wasn't blushing as she opened the door.

He smiled at her. "Have these ladies been embarrassing you with their bawdy stories, Molly?"

"We tried, but she wouldn't cooperate. She told us she had seen more naked men than we had," Ada said.

Molly blinked at the audacious lie and at the fact that Ada probably knew Molly had seen more than she should have. She could feel her face warming even more.

"I—well, I—" Molly began.

"Shh," Seth said near her ear. "Forget the naked men. I thought I woke up and smelled chocolate chip cookies."

Molly pointed to the plate of cookies.

"In my apartment," he clarified, whispering near her ear.

Ah, now she understood, and there was no way she was going to admit that she had been watching him while he lay naked under a blanket. "They're very potent, aromatic cookies," she said, defiantly lifting her chin.

"You're cute when you lie," he told her, and she blushed and looked away to hide the blush. *Had* she lied a great deal lately? Well, she was certainly guilty of sins of omission.

He turned her back to him with one finger tucked under her chin. "That was probably the wrong thing to say. I'll take you home in a minute," he told her. "No cleaning today." Thank goodness. She wasn't sure she could face his apartment again today. The memories of him—and those photos—were still too fresh in her mind.

"Thank you. Just let me go change Ruthie's diaper." She turned and looked at Ada, who was holding Ruthie, and found the woman studying her intently, a serious expression in her eyes.

But Ada shook her head and smiled, holding out the baby.

* * *

"What are you thinking, Ada?" Seth asked when Molly had left the room.

"Not much, just pondering Molly. She's a delight to have around. And she still reminds me of someone I might have known once. When she turned her head there for a minute, the curve of her jaw, that nose, those eyelashes...I don't know. Something's just not right."

"You bet. The fact that you haven't offered me a cookie yet is what's not right." Seth moved closer.

Ada held out the plate, but he leaned closer still. Cecily, Dora and Fran were talking to each other, but he knew they heard more than they let on.

"Ada..." He lowered his voice, not to a whisper, because that would have called attention. Instead, he held out a cookie as if he were discussing its texture. But that wasn't what he had in mind. He understood what Ada was saying. He was so afraid for Molly that he had considered checking into her background himself, but then he remembered her fear of reporters. "Leave it, Ada," he warned. "I don't know what's in her past, but whatever it is, she doesn't want to go there again. If you push it, you might hurt her."

"I wouldn't. She's a doll."

"You wouldn't do it intentionally, but you love a mystery. This is not Matlock, Ada. It's Molly's life."

"You know that I don't spread tales." She quickly glanced toward her friends. "But I can't help wondering."

"Then wonder. Just don't wonder out loud anymore."

At the sound of Ruthie's laughter and Molly's hushed tones laced with love for her daughter, Ada sighed. "You're right. I guess I have too much time on my hands."

"You care," he told her, and he touched her wrinkled fingers. "Now give me another cookie, so I can keep my energy up and get Molly home."

"Reprobate," she told him, but she handed him a cookie.

"Don't you forget it." And he strolled into the next room in search of Molly.

"Almost ready?" he asked her, and she looked up at him and smiled. It hit him right between the eyes, that smile. It hit him in the chest, in the heart, it seared his lungs, it sent heat surging through him.

It was just a smile, he wanted to protest, but he knew he was wrong. Molly's smile was different; it was unforgettable.

She had hinted that someone was looking for her. That smile would be a dead giveaway. He had to protect her, and fast.

If he didn't...

Don't think about it, he told himself. Just show her what she has to do, and pray that she can do it when the time comes.

He smiled at her and held out his hand. "Let's go. It's time for another night of lessons."

Chapter 14

Shannon had seen him again—that cute, clean-cut guy who seemed interested in Seth. This time she had nearly sneaked up on him as he was trying to follow Seth and that woman. Who was that woman, anyway? She had to know.

But for now, the woman worried Shannon less than the guy who was trailing Seth. Or trying to. Mr. Cleancut had lost Seth and the woman when they had done some serious zigzagging.

Her brother was good, Shannon had to admit. But she was better. Even though she had only lived on the streets of San Francisco for about a year, she had been forced to sneak around in order to keep from calling attention to herself.

She had been successful…most of the time.

A grimace crossed her face. Anxiety made her heart race. "That's old news," she told herself. "Drop it. Just pay attention to Mr. Preppy. He's up to no good."

She studied him as he wandered down the street, peering into every doorway, every alleyway. Nice butt, she couldn't help noticing.

Don't do that, she told herself. Just figure out what he's doing here, try to find out what he's up to.

He turned suddenly and she quickly slid under a brick overhang, hiding in the shadows.

Almost caught. It was as if he knew she was there.

Not likely, she thought. A guy like that—what could he know about spying?

Not much. When she finally decided it was safe to come out, the guy was already gone. He had missed her, hadn't he?

Maybe, but he wants something pretty bad. It was Seth he was interested in, too. She had seen him that time following her brother, and she had wanted to yell to Seth to watch out. Not that warning Seth was why she had been there that day. No, sometimes she just felt the need to see him for a minute or two. Even if just from a distance.

Her heart hurt. She reminded herself that she had long ago given up the right to be Seth's sister. He checked up on her now and then, sometimes he sent money, but that was because Seth was a good person. Duty was part of his genetic code. What's more, he had always been a good brother and she had never been a good sister. Hadn't done a darn thing for him.

Now she could, even if he would never know. In addition to tailing the woman, she could keep her eye on Mr. Gorgeous Preppy and make sure he didn't do Seth any harm.

"Just take one false step, buddy, and I'll be all over you with everything I've got," she whispered. But the comment ended up making her feel all the wrong things.

He really was far too attractive a man for this part of town. Probably had a beautiful debutante girlfriend, one who would give him beautiful debutante babies.

"Well, that's just fine," she said, sticking her chin up and marching back toward her apartment. "Don't think you'll be getting any from me."

Which was just too stupid a comment to make. The guy was probably a real blue-eyed jerk. What's more, she'd never even met him, and he didn't know that she existed. And if he did, he would do the smart thing and hit the road fast.

Molly stood in her living room, face-to-face with Seth. Ruthie was sleeping in the next room, which was probably a good thing. Seth was about to transform himself into someone Ruthie had never seen before.

"All right, I'm an attacker, Molly. What do you do?"

"I run?"

"Good. If you can, you get away. What if you can't? What if I'm on top of you?"

His words caught her by surprise. Her breath hitched in her throat, and it wasn't fear that was foremost in her mind.

Seth advanced a step, his eyes dark and intent. "Molly?"

She swallowed hard and tried to think of Seth as her attacker, not a potential lover. "If he doesn't have a gun or a knife, I resist letting him take me anywhere. I use the weapons I already have at my disposal," she answered. "My legs, my fingernails, my voice."

"Exactly," he coached, and then he showed her how to bend a man's thumb backward and put him at a disadvantage, how to stomp on an attacker's instep. He encouraged her to box a man's ears, to kick him in the shins or groin, to poke him in the eye or chop him in the throat. If she had to, she could pinch an attacker hard on the upper inner thigh or underarm, bend his first two fingers backward, anything to inflict enough pain to buy time.

"Remember, I'm an attacker. I want to rob or hurt you. Come disarm me," he warned, and she threw herself at him, time and time again. She pretended he was Kevin and she did what he had taught her to do.

"Good," he told her when she had finally brought him to his knees with the backward finger move. Slowly, almost casually, he slid his hand into his back pocket. It was a movement that looked natural, but somehow Molly didn't think it was.

"Oh, I've hurt you." Suddenly he was Seth again, not

Kevin at all, not even some man pretending to harm her. She knelt and reached behind him to pull his injured fingers out…and realized that doing so brought her up against his chest.

"Molly," he growled. "You didn't hurt me at all. And I'm not Seth for now. I'm a predator."

"Not anymore. Now you're hurt," she said. "Let me see," and she reached again, her arm slipping behind his back.

His body went rigid. She looked up.

"Molly, don't…" he warned, and then he was the one snaking his arm behind her back. He pulled her to him and then his lips came down on hers. He brushed back and forth over her mouth. And then he settled in and tasted her fully, his mouth hard and firm and warm.

She shivered in his grasp and moved closer.

They were thigh to thigh, his chest hard against her breasts, his mouth plundering hers.

He was warm and aroused and…Seth. She couldn't get enough and so she angled her head, trying to taste more of him. She raked her palms over his back.

Seth pulled her tighter. "You make me insane," he whispered. "I want—"

"What?"

"This. You." And he slid his hand up between them. He cupped her breast with one hand, curved his other palm around her thigh.

Heat seared her. A moan slid from her throat. She was so afraid he would stop touching her.

His thumb slid over her nipple and she arced against him—helplessly. Eager, open, vulnerable. Molly cried out, tears misting her eyes.

She had been alone for what felt like forever, and this was Seth. Her need was so great it was painful.

His name slipped from her lips on a soft moan, and she knew that she was ready to give everything to him, open herself to him, surrender it all.

The word *surrender* was like an explosion in her head. If she did this, if she continued, she would be completely vulnerable. The thought assailed her though she tried to ignore it and only feel the pleasure, to concentrate only on Seth and his touch.

And yet, she couldn't do this. She could not be vulnerable again. If he touched her even one more time, she would be unable to stop. And then, once she had surrendered, once she had known what making love with Seth could be like, how could she survive?

She wanted tomorrow, but there would be no tomorrow for her and Seth. He wasn't that kind of man, and she was on the run. At any time she might have to leave without so much as a goodbye. And she couldn't even explain any of this without endangering Seth. She didn't know what he would do, but if she dragged him in, she was sure that Kevin would go after him with all the power he could muster. That scared her to death. Kevin didn't like anyone interfering with his plans.

Not knowing how she found the willpower or made

the effort, she took a deep breath and pushed against Seth. Slowly he released her. He let her go.

"I'm sorry," she said, her voice weak.

He knelt there, staring at her, his chest heaving with the effort. And then he shook his head. "No, you were right. This wasn't supposed to happen." He smoothed her hair, gently touched her face and set her aside.

"I was supposed to be teaching you," he reminded her. "Not tumbling you backward onto the floor and having my way with you. This wasn't part of the lesson. Are you all right?"

She nodded, but now she felt panic climbing inside her. There was so little she knew about Seth, but she knew this much—he had a strong sense of responsibility. He thought he'd hurt her. She couldn't allow that.

So she scrambled up beside him as he rose. Ignoring all the warnings she had just given herself, she leaned close and kissed him lightly. Just once.

"You need to know that I really wanted you to kiss me, to touch me. I wanted even more, and you can believe it's true, because if I hadn't wanted it you would have been lying on the ground with a concussion. I have a very good self-defense teacher, buster, and I don't take my lessons lightly." She plastered a slightly teary but wide fake smile on her face.

Seth chuckled. "Nice try, princess, but I don't buy it. A self-defense teacher does not make a move on his student. You should have gone for the concussion. I mean that."

He turned to go. "You did well, today," he told her. "You'll know enough soon. You won't need me anymore."

And if that were true, she wondered, once he had gone, why did she have such a terrible overpowering urge to chase him down the street and tell him that she had been wrong. She *could* handle making love with him.

Except she wasn't quite sure that she could. No doubt she would never find out now.

It was early evening of the next day, and Molly had left Ruthie in Ada's care while she headed for the local drugstore. Ada's bunions were hurting her, and Molly had volunteered to go for first aid.

But it wasn't first aid she was thinking about. It was Seth. In spite of her best efforts, she couldn't seem to forget how it had felt to be held against his body, how warm his skin was, how his mouth had made her dissolve.

Then she heard it, just the tiniest scrape behind her right shoulder. Probably nothing, she told herself, even as fear crept in. What, after all, had she been thinking, daydreaming about Seth? Hadn't he taught her to remain aware of her surroundings?

Molly took a deep breath and kept walking. All right, shake it off, you're aware now, she reminded herself. Listen. Pay attention.

She did. The step was very faint, almost indiscernible from the other city sounds, but it was there. Light. A kid, a small man, perhaps. Through accident or intent, someone was timing his footsteps to her own.

What should she do? Where should she go? Not back to Ada's. She didn't want to lead a stalker to her friends. Was that Kevin behind her? No, Kevin wouldn't be so light-footed. Maybe it was nothing, no one important. She needed to know.

And then she had an idea. Turning, she continued to walk, always listening for the steps behind her. She moved down two blocks and then she turned again, making her way by Mr. Alex's. He would be gone already, but he lit his shop well, even at night, and he polished the glass until it reflected everything.

Molly forced herself to maintain her pace, to wait, never to turn, until she reached the far end of the long glass panel.

Then she glanced to the side and back. The woman had just entered her field of vision. Whirling, Molly caught a flash of blond as the woman slid into the shadows beneath an awning.

Not quickly enough, Molly thought. I know this place. And she knew that there were no spaces between the buildings here. To get out, the woman would have to either move forward or backward down the street.

Molly closed in cautiously. She could barely hear the other woman breathing. For a minute, she wasn't sure she was even there. Had she been wrong? Had the woman found a way out?

Clutching her purse, Molly felt for the key chain she kept there—the one with the pepper spray and the small flashlight.

"Who are you?" she asked, moving forward. "And why are you following me?"

No answer. And then Molly clicked her light on and arced it in the same moment. What she saw almost made her stumble—blond hair, gray eyes, a face she had seen before, even though this one was older.

"You're…Seth's…" she said on a breath.

The woman's eyes narrowed. "Hell no. He tell you that?" Her voice was hard, but her lips trembled ever so slightly.

Molly shook her head. "He didn't tell me anything. I saw your picture. You have his eyes." Molly took a step forward, and the woman started to skid away.

"I won't hurt you," Molly said.

The other woman laughed. "Lady, just hope I don't hurt you. I'm betting I know a lot more about how to make a person pay than you do. I could stomp you into the ground and grind you beneath my stilettos and call it a good day. You? You look too prissy to get blood on your hands."

"Why would you hurt me?"

"Why wouldn't I? You look to be easy pickings. My brother hitting on you? Or maybe not. Maybe you're the one hitting on him?" There was an edge to her voice.

Ah, so Seth wasn't the only protector in the family.

"Neither," Molly said slowly. "Seth's just helping me."

"Hah! Helping you what?"

Molly wasn't sure how much she wanted to tell this woman with the dark, angry eyes. She was Seth's sister, and she obviously wanted to know what Molly's relationship to him was, but she was never around. Something wasn't right.

"Seth is teaching me to defend myself, so that people can't sneak up on me. He's just being a good citizen, a protector." She stared directly into the woman's eyes and thought she saw a flash of pain.

"Yeah, that's Seth." The woman's voice cracked slightly. "Always the protector." The vulnerable look fled. "Some women might take advantage of that."

Molly nodded. "I wouldn't. It's not that way. He's just…good to everyone."

"Not that I care what the two of you do," the woman said, and she turned to go. "Seth and I don't talk. We don't see each other anymore."

"Maybe you should," Molly answered, but the woman acted as if she hadn't heard. She kept walking until she disappeared into the falling darkness.

Molly waited until she had gone and then she moved down the street herself.

From a doorway leading to an upstairs apartment, a man stepped into the street. Jeff Payton watched as the brown-haired woman walked away. He knew that since she was the one who was spending all her time with Seth McCabe, she was the one with the story to tell, the one who might give him a lead. A professional would stay with her and see if she gave up any secrets.

But a mere man—now he wasn't always that predictable. And the spunky little blonde with the ponytail and the pretty eyes intrigued him. She fascinated him in totally inappropriate ways. It was surely a bad idea to mix his kind of business with pleasure.

Still he turned and moved off in the direction the blond woman had gone. Seth McCabe's story was getting more interesting all the time.

But despite his mission, it wasn't really McCabe that he wanted to talk to right now. It was his sister, if he could believe the conversation that had just taken place.

"She's long gone, Payton," he whispered to himself. "Forget it."

But she would be back. Like him, she'd been hanging around too much lately to give up so easily. And when she returned, he would find out more about her.

Chapter 15

Seth knew something was different the minute Molly opened her door to him the next day. She let him in right away, but she was studying him as if he were a total stranger, one she was concerned about. Worry lines formed between her eyes. She looked tired, as if she hadn't slept well.

Fear gnawed at him even though he fought to keep it at bay. "What's wrong?" he asked.

She shook her head, giving him a brief smile. "Nothing. I'm probably just a little tired. Ruthie had a restless night."

"But she's all right?" He couldn't keep from worrying about the little one. She was such a happy baby that he couldn't imagine her having a bad night.

"She's fine. I think she got a little overexcited over at Ada's. Even babies this young react to a change in their routines." She turned aside and started fiddling with a torn place in the curtains.

"So you're okay with this?" he asked. "I can come back another time. We don't have to have a lesson tonight."

"Trying to get rid of me, Seth?"

"Of course not."

She turned and gave him a grin. "Good, because it wouldn't work. I want to learn to be tough. I want you to teach me everything you know—how to be fearless, how to be unreadable, how to be less squeamish about drawing blood if I'm ever forced to. I want you to show me what you already have a handle on—how to strike fear into the hearts of the bad guys."

Seth flinched inside. It wasn't always about striking fear into the hearts of others but in controlling your own fear. And he did have fears. The truth was that he couldn't deal with the thought of ever being responsible for anyone ever again, but he had no intention of telling her that. She needed reassurance if she was going to face all the bad things that lurked in the shadows. If there was anyone else around who could give her that, he would step aside gladly, but there apparently wasn't. For now, he was the best she had. Heaven help him if he failed her.

"All right, today you show me everything you keep in your purse, and I show you how to make the most of it."

"My purse?"

He grinned. "This is where you decide if I'm trust-worthy enough to find out that you carry cartoon-character bandages with you."

She wrinkled her nose. "Plain old flesh-colored ones, I'm afraid. I'm not very exciting."

Oh, she was so wrong. Every time she turned her head, every time she smiled, every time she looked at him, he got shaky inside. He was on the verge of engaging in some very unwise actions, mostly dealing with trying to get her naked skin against his. Molly Delavan was more excitement than he might be capable of handling.

"Spill it," he said. "I promise not to pass judgment."

She did. He had expected to find cute little trinkets, tubes of makeup, odds and ends no man would ever think of carrying around with him. Wasn't that the kind of thing all women carried? He'd seen Ada pull entire medicine cabinets from her purse, half the contents of an antique store, and ten colors of lipstick when she never wore lipstick. And his sister had always had some cute little gadgets tucked away, plenty of stuff that per-sonalized the contents of her purse.

Molly had the basics—a thin wallet, a comb, a few tissues, a pen and pencil and the always present key/pep-per spray/flashlight that was attached to her purse. That was it. Nothing that shouted "Molly" to the world. Molly was vibrant and caring. She put flowers in jelly glasses, set out decorations for his table. Yet, there wasn't a whit of her personality in that bag. She just wasn't there.

That worried him more than anything. He had suspected that she had secrets. Now he wondered just how dangerous those secrets were. He would bet his career that she wasn't a criminal, but he didn't know who she was. She had a mailbox with no name on it, she had no telephone and, apparently, she didn't socialize with anyone other than himself and Ada, which didn't count, damn it. He didn't know what she had come from or what had driven her here.

He couldn't ask. She didn't want him to know, and he knew better than to pry. Shannon's experience had taught him well. And besides, who was he to talk? He had his own secret life.

Something wasn't right, but she wouldn't thank him for mentioning that. He should get on with today's lesson.

"Okay," he finally said, and considered his next words.

He glanced up and caught her studying him again, with eyes as sad as any he'd ever seen.

All thought of lessons flew right out the window. He walked over to her, placed his hands on her shoulders. "Tell me," he said.

She flinched. "What?"

Seth smoothed back her hair. "Something's worrying you. It's so obvious, and, to tell you the truth, you're scaring the hell out of me. Just tell me this much. Did someone try to hurt you? Some kid ringing your doorbell again? Some dirtbag following you?"

She looked away.

"Molly? Please. I don't want to overstep the boundaries here, but this much I have to know." And he would beat the crap out of the guy who scared her this way...if only she would tell him what had happened.

"I...I met your sister." Her voice was so very quiet, but he heard her clearly. His hands froze on her shoulders. His fingers clenched hard, making her jump.

Immediately he pulled away. He ran one hand through his hair. "Shannon?"

"You have more than one?"

"No. Just Shannon."

"I—it's none of my business, I know."

He didn't dispute that. In truth, he didn't know what to say. So he said what was rushing through his head. "Where? How?"

"On the street."

"Just like that. On the street."

She didn't look away this time. "Yes. I thought you should know."

He leaned against the wall. "All right. All right, then. Yes, I have a sister. She's twenty-two, five years younger than I am."

She waited, but he couldn't speak. What could he tell her? Anything he could say would bring the pain back. He didn't want anyone's pity and he knew darn well that pity was what Molly would feel. Moreover, he had lived his history. He didn't want to talk about it.

"We're estranged," he said. "She lives in the city. We don't speak."

Molly opened her mouth, but he shook his head. "Leave it, Molly. You have to. Please. This is the way Shannon and I want things, so I want you to just leave it."

She nodded, and then, her hands shaking, she reached for her purse. "Teach me what you came for," she said. "Ruthie could be at risk. I need to know now."

Dominic threw the pictures down in front of Kevin. "What do you think?"

Kevin took the pictures in his hands. He leaned back in his chair and held the photos up to the light. "Grainy," he said.

"It was dark. There were other people around. My man couldn't get close."

"I can't tell anything from these. These are total crap. I don't like crap."

"So what do you want?"

"I want you to find out if that's Molly. I'm not taking someone off the street who isn't. Mistakes aren't acceptable."

"I'll get more pictures."

"Do better than that. Get closer, and get me some hard information on the kid. That's real important. That's what I need if I'm going to get custody. It's what *you* need if you want to stay out of the graveyard and get paid."

"Okay. I'll try."

"Do more than try. Get proof. Get close. And don't

come back if you don't have something I can really
use."

"If I get that, I get paid?"

"If you get that and I decide that she's the one, then
you get another job. Then you get paid."

"What's the other job?"

"What do you think, you idiot? The next job is bringing her and the brat to me."

Molly was on her way home from cleaning up at
Ada's. Seth had still been asleep, and she hadn't seen
him, but that didn't mean he was out of her thoughts.

"It hurt him to talk about his sister, Ruthie. It hurt
Shannon to talk about him, too. Sounds like there's a
lot of history there, some bad stuff, but…some good
stuff, too. Not that they're going to admit it. What a
waste. The good stuff is so hard to find."

And for a moment, a horrible sense of longing threatened to overcome Molly. She and her aunt had had the
good stuff. Aunt Louisa had been strict, but she had
loved her niece. It had been several years since her death.

"I wish she could see you, sweetie. She would have
adored you. Having family that cares is so important.
Seth's sister cares about him—they both seem so alone.
Maybe I could help somehow."

More likely she would just make things worse. It
wasn't her right to interfere. If anyone tried to dig into
her personal secrets right now, she would be horrified.
But Seth wasn't Kevin, and she wasn't Shannon.

"I won't do much," she said to her daughter. But the longing to make things right for Seth was so strong. She would give a lot to see him smile like he had in that picture in his room. And she was very certain that a large part of the reason Seth seldom smiled had something to do with Shannon. "Maybe if I could talk to Shannon once more, I could help in some way." Surely talking to the woman one more time wouldn't hurt.

But all thought of Shannon fled when Molly let herself into her apartment building. The front door, the only door to her apartment was partially kicked in and footsteps were clattering down the hall toward the rear entrance to the building.

For two seconds Molly stood there in shock. Then, without thinking, her heart thumping erractically, she ran in the direction of the footsteps, but the back door was standing open, the curtains in the nearby window blowing in the draft. There was no one in sight.

She wandered back to her door and stared at the hole there. She touched the partially splintered wood and felt her throat completely closing up. Her heart was a bass drum. Her shoes were nailed to the floor. Nausea threatened to choke her.

What to do? What to do? Fear gushed through her wildly. Confusion filled her soul. Only two coherent thoughts sifted through. *Get out. Get Seth.*

Molly tried to act. She closed her eyes. If there had been a visible intruder, maybe she could have put Seth's lessons to use. Certainly she would have fought heaven and hell for Ruthie. But this invasion with no target left her shaking and impotent. It didn't escape her notice that, while her door wasn't the first one in the apartment building hallway, it was the only one that had been attacked.

As if *she* were the actual target.

Suddenly she sucked in a huge, gasping breath. She turned and ran. Wildly, blindly. "Don't worry, Ruthie," she somehow managed to say through chattering teeth. "Mom will take care of things."

Then she shut up and ran. The trip to Ada's was a blind rush down the street. Who knew what she passed or who she nearly ran down? All she knew was that Ada's was sanctuary. Seth was there.

She only stopped at Ada's long enough to tell her that she needed to talk to Seth and to ask her to watch Ruthie. To her credit, Ada didn't ask questions about Molly's windblown hair or her frantic demeanor. She just held out her arms for the baby.

Then Molly was stumbling up the stairs instead. With shaking fingers, she shoved her key into the door and let herself in. With boldness she would never have possessed in other circumstances, she rapped once on Seth's bedroom door and let herself in.

He had turned on his side, already awake. No doubt she had made a lot of noise. But when she burst into the room, he tucked the sheet around his waist and rose.

"Molly?"

She pressed her fingers to her lips. "I'm sorry. I know

all your lessons. I should have remembered what to do, but Ruthie was there and I was afraid for her. Someone had been in the apartment building. They—someone broke my door. I was afraid they might still be there. What should I have done?"

Swearing beneath his breath, he strode toward her and kept coming, moving up to her and wrapping her in his embrace. She could feel him take a deep, shuddery breath. "You did exactly what you should have done," he said. "You got out."

"Yes, but the apartment…I didn't even look."

"You didn't need to. It's just stuff. Not your life or Ruthie's. Running is the right thing to do a lot of the time. People don't get credit for that." He released her and took a step back. He took her chin in his hand and nudged her head up until she was staring into his eyes. "You did what needed to be done. Anything else would have been foolish and risky."

She nodded slightly, but her body was still tense. She was on the verge of shaking apart.

"Molly, hon, tell me something."

"What?"

"Could you have done anything to stop this?"

"I locked my doors and windows. I know I did."

"Exactly. So it wasn't your fault."

She looked at him.

He stroked his warm fingers over her cold cheek. "Say it."

"What?" Her voice came out on a choked whisper.

"Say, I did everything I could. This was not my fault."

She opened her mouth and closed it again.

"You need to say it," he urged. "I need to hear you say it. Honey, you're breakin' my heart here."

And that was what it took. She lifted her chin and stood on her own. "I—I did everything I could," she said, even if her voice was a bit weak. "This break-in was not my fault." Her voice grew firmer on the last line.

Seth gave her a half smile. "You're sure as hell right about that. Some jerk tried to make his life easier, but then that's the way of jerks. They'll steal your self-esteem while they try to steal your television. Don't let them win that way. You're better than they are. You are, Molly. So much better." And he leaned forward and kissed her on the top of her head.

Her breath *whooshed* out in a gentle flow. She didn't think of what she had left behind at the apartment, only of Seth's strength, only of the fact that Ruthie was still safe.

"What now?" she asked.

"Now," he said gently. "You go stay with Ada while I get dressed and go check things out. Then we make a police report for starters."

Panic catapulted through Molly at lightning speed. She struggled to think of something to say that wouldn't sound suspicious and couldn't come up with a single thing. Finally, she simply closed her eyes.

"Seth?"

"What?"

"I'll get out so you can get dressed, but I'm going with you when you go."

He started to argue. She stepped close and placed her palm gently over his lips. "I have to. I need to."

She pulled her hand away and was gifted with one of his fiercest looks. "All right, but I don't like it."

"Okay." But if he didn't like that, what was he going to think of what she planned to say next? "And I don't want to call the police," she said. The very thought made her want to keel over. She felt physically ill. "I don't have anything worth stealing, so nothing of value was taken, and whoever was responsible is probably long gone."

He opened his mouth to protest.

"What if it got in the police blotter in the newspapers?" she asked, rushing on. "Then everyone would know that I'm a woman living alone." Which was the truth, but only half of the truth.

That did it. He closed his mouth.

"All right, then," he said. "Go talk to Ada. I'll get dressed and then we'll go."

She nodded and turned to leave.

"But Molly?"

She looked back over her shoulder. His dark hair hung about his bare shoulders. With his sheet slipping low on his hips, he was all muscle and male. She bit her lip and waited.

"I'm staying at your place tonight," he said. "And that's nonnegotiable."

Chapter 16

Seth did a circuit of Molly's apartment, checking all the locks on the windows and doors. For the first time in several years he would not go out on the streets.

Instead he would be closed up in this small apartment with Molly.

His breath hitched, his gut clenched, his body felt as if a small heater had been turned on inside him. How was he going to make it through the night?

By remembering why you're here, buddy, he told himself. By thinking of Molly and Ruthie first and forgetting that Molly makes you want to beg for her to touch you with just the tip of one finger. That would be enough.

Liar. If she touched him in any way, he would grab

her just as he had before. And this time, with both their emotions so near the surface, they might not be able to stop.

"Ruthie's in bed," Molly said from behind him, and Seth turned to look at her. The small night-light in the single bedroom let out a glow that captured Molly and turned her golden, like a fairy creature from a children's story.

Except Molly was real. And there was a hell of a lot of night they had to traverse together before morning came.

He was already rock hard. This was never going to work.

"What do you and Ruthie do every night?" he asked. Better to talk of nothing than to think of what he'd like to be doing.

Molly smiled. "Well, generally speaking, Ruthie's not into a lot of variety, but she's not real choosy about what we do, either. An infant has her limits, you know. She likes to listen to the radio or to my off-key singing."

"But you sing, anyway, because she likes it, don't you?"

She tossed her head. "Hey, I'm a mom. We do what we can."

"What else?"

She smiled. "Well, sometimes things get especially exciting and I tell her a story. Or we get out the blocks and pretend we're architects. Build the Leaning Tower of Pisa, that kind of thing. We're just a bundle of excitement around here in our spare time."

Which got to him, because he knew that they didn't have much spare time. Molly worked all day and then she came to help Ada. She was probably dead tired by the time she got home. And tonight, when she needed her sleep, here he was bugging her about how she spent her free time. Because he didn't want to have to think about sleeping in the same space as her.

"Ruthie's in bed. You need your sleep, too."

Immediately she looked tense. "I don't think I can."

"Because of what happened to your door or because of me?"

She blushed. "You don't scare me, Seth."

Which wasn't exactly what he meant and she knew it. But he wouldn't go there. He wanted her to relax. "Now you've gone and done it," he said. "You've wounded my masculine pride. I've got a reputation as a badass to uphold. Are you messing with that, Delavan?"

Molly suddenly gave him a slow, speculative smile. "A badass? Hey, McCabe, just because you look tough doesn't mean you *are* tough." Which was the closest she had ever come to mentioning his scars. He liked the fact that she had plowed right in without shying away from it.

"I'm very tough," he said. "So tough that I'm going to lie down on this couch here, facing the door, and if anyone even tries to get in here, I'll be down his throat so far, he'll choke to death."

"Oh, no, Seth, you're helping me. You can't sleep on the couch. I'll do that."

Oh, yeah, like he could sleep in her bed and not dream about making love with her.

"I don't like beds," he said. "Too prissy."

"Prissy? That's what your sister called me."

That nearly stopped him short. "It's a family thing. We don't do comfort. Shannon was always sneaking out to sleep in the family tree house where I had set up a lumpy cot. Now, are you going to your room to sleep or am I going to have to strip down right here in front of you?" He reached for the first button on his shirt.

For a second she stood there, and his body turned molten. Maybe she *was* going to stand there.

She looked up at him. "So, you're going to sleep on the couch, and you don't want any arguments."

"That's about it."

"You think I'm still too soft for anything but a bed, don't you?"

"Molly, I'm just trying to keep my hands off of you tonight. Which is why it would be best if you lock yourself in the bedroom while I set up camp here on the couch. We've both agreed that it would be best if we don't chase down whatever happens whenever we get too close."

Molly looked as if she still wanted to argue, but she raised a shoulder in acquiescence. "All right. Just let me get you a blanket and a pillow."

Which wasn't necessary, because he wasn't really going to get any sleep. But she didn't need to know that, and she *did* need to think that he was fine with the situation. If she woke up in the middle of the night and started worrying about what would happen the next time someone tried to break in to her place, he wanted her to at least get some rest before the middle-of-the-night demons stole her sanity. He knew all too well about the haunting thoughts that arose at three in the morning. They were his old enemies. It was better to face them with at least a bit of shut-eye in your system.

So he took the pillow and blanket she offered. He tried not to listen as she went into the next room, shut the door and proceeded to remove her clothing. Or at least, he imagined that was what she was doing.

Seth forced himself to keep breathing normally, to keep himself away from that door. Because imagination was great for a writer, but it was hell for a man intent on keeping his hands off a naked woman.

He hoped like heck that morning came soon. If he could get through tonight, tomorrow he would set Molly up with a bodyguard. And then everything would be all right.

The night felt as if it were a century long. Molly was chased by restless dreams of Kevin demanding that she give over his money, and when she looked to where he was pointing, she saw only Ruthie wrapped in a blanket made out of hundred-dollar bills. Kevin snatched Ruthie up and ran, pushing through the hole in her door, and Molly cried out, knowing she would never again see her child outside of movies or magazine ads. Ruthie would grow up being valued only for her face and the money she could bring in. She would never be allowed to be a real person.

Molly came half-awake. She schooled herself to relax. Eventually she outran the nightmare and drifted off.

And then it began once more.

Kevin went through the whole process again, breaking in, stealing Ruthie. Frantically, Molly tried to stop him, but he was too fast. He was laughing all the way.

Then, just as Kevin was almost away, Seth stepped in front of him. He looked invincible, strong, determined. He looked like everything she trusted, all that she wanted. For a second, she thought everything would be all right…until Kevin pulled a knife.

Molly stopped breathing. She tried to scream, to beg Kevin to stop, to convince Seth to run.

Kevin plunged the knife into Seth.

Molly sat up, breathing hard, feeling wild and lost and unsure of what had just happened. She clutched the damp tangled sheets.

It had just been a dream, a crazy dream. But silly as it was, she felt an indefinable need to check on Ruthie. Not that that was unusual. She checked on Ruthie all the time. Probably other mothers did that, too.

That was usual, but she also felt a need to check on Seth, and that was something else entirely.

She fought the feeling. Seth was sleeping on the couch. He had boarded up her broken door, good and tight, so it was silly to think anything might have actually happened. Besides, if she went out there, she might wake him, and he had made it clear he wanted her to stay in her room.

She leaned back against the pillows, coaching herself to settle down and try to get back to sleep.

Then, somewhere in the night, a board creaked. Her heart started pounding.

Another board creaked.

Too bad if she was acting crazy. She shoved back the sheets and climbed out of bed. Carefully she pushed open the door and moved into the living room, looking toward the couch.

Seth wasn't there.

She turned and saw him, in a chair by the window, looking out into the dark that was lit only by the streetlights. He usually worked at night. No doubt he was having trouble sleeping.

But he was very still. If he had fallen asleep, he would get cold. She picked up the blanket from the couch and slowly moved toward him.

"Don't do that." His deep voice broke the stillness.

She almost dropped the blanket. "I'm sorry. I thought you were asleep, but—you're missing work tonight because of me. I shouldn't have let you come."

"Work can wait. You had a traumatic experience today. You need to know you aren't alone, that you and Ruthie are safe."

And she realized that despite her dream, she did feel safe. Because Seth had sacrificed for her yet again.

"Have you always worked at night?" she asked.

At first there was only silence. Then he shifted slightly. "For a long time. It suits me."

"Night always seems like the loneliest time of day for me."

"I'm not denying that, sunshine lady."

"Me?"

"You. You're not meant for darkness."

"You're not dark, not in the way you mean."

He laughed. "There you go again, looking on the bright side. That's a morning person for you...or at least that's you."

"There's nothing wrong with being a morning person."

"Not at all." He turned and looked toward her, but with the streetlight drifting in from behind him, his face was in shadow, hers was in light. She felt exposed, and she tried not to think about the fact that she was standing there wearing nothing more than a thin T-shirt.

Trying didn't work. Caught in Seth's gaze, she felt desire begin to unfurl within her. It wasn't just because it had been a long time since she had been touched, either, although that had something to do with it. No, it was him more than anything. She simply wanted Seth.

"There's nothing wrong with darkness, either," she said. "Sometimes it's an advantage."

She took a step toward him.

"You don't want to do that," he told her.

Perhaps he was right. She stopped. She could turn

and run now and go back to her bedroom, alone and cold. She could dream of Kevin again.

A shiver ripped through her.

"Damn it, Molly," Seth said, and then he was beside her. "Don't let me do this."

But it was too late. She didn't know exactly what he was going to do, but she knew that she wanted him to do it.

"I don't want to be alone tonight," she said.

For a minute, she thought he was going to swear, that he was going to retreat or order her back to her room. She could feel the tension radiating off his body.

"This is probably the worst idea I've ever had," he said. And then he swooped in, sliding his hand behind her head, his mouth descending on hers. He was warm, he was strong, and for this moment and this moment alone, he was hers to touch.

She touched him, just sliding her palm up his bare chest.

His heart pounded hard and strong beneath her fingertips. He scooped her up, blanket and all, and carried her toward the couch, standing there for a minute. "I don't want you to regret this," he whispered.

Her answer was to drop the blanket onto the couch. "I won't," she promised, although she didn't know if that were actually true. She only knew that she had to have him. "I want you with me tonight, Seth," she whispered. "Please."

"Heaven help me, yes," he said, lowering her to the

couch and following her down. He braced himself over her, his hair falling forward. She breathed in the scent of him and reached up to touch his face, loving the rough texture of his jaw.

Seth turned his head and kissed her palm. "You haunt my nights," he told her, and then he kissed her again, deeply this time. "You're almost too bright to touch."

"No, I'm not. I'm like any other woman. Touch me."

For a moment he gazed at her in the darkness.

"You're not like any other woman. You don't have to be. What you have to be is sure that you want this."

Her answer was to slide her palms up to his shoulders and offer him her lips.

Seth groaned and took them, his mouth meeting hers in a harsh, demanding kiss that stole her breath and any sanity she might ever have possessed. He made love to her mouth, brushing, nibbling, nipping. His taste was dark and sweet and wild, like the night he favored.

Molly met him kiss for kiss, unable to get enough of his touch. Her breasts felt tight and painful. Now that she had turned her back on caution, she wanted all of him against all of her. Her thin T-shirt felt heavy, wrong.

She pulled at it, but he was there before her, sweeping his palms up her thighs, beneath the cloth and slipping it off her. Now she was exposed, every inch of her except the small scrap of her lace panties. Then he stripped that away, and every bit of protection she had was gone.

And she was suddenly aware that her body was that of a woman who had borne a child only two months ago. Her breasts were fuller, half-laden with milk, her tummy no longer flat.

"Oh." She dragged in a breath and instinctively held one arm over herself as if that could keep him from seeing, especially with the pale beam of the streetlight shining through the slats in the blinds and revealing all of her flaws.

"Molly?" Seth's voice shook. His hands were shaking, too, but he stopped.

"I have…stretch marks," she told him, and he dipped his head and kissed her abdomen. Sensation ripped through her body, her breasts tingling. She moaned and arced up off the couch.

"They're beautiful. You got them in a noble cause, giving Ruthie life. I have burn marks," Seth said, and he flipped her over gently, ending up beneath her. Now the dim streetlight was on him, revealing his beautiful, strong body with its scars—on his shoulders, down one arm, across part of his chest. She had seen him without his shirt, before. The scars had been there, but she had seen only Seth. Now she saw another part of Seth, the man who had suffered.

"Your scars are a part of your history, too. Let me touch." And she leaned over him and kissed her way from his shoulder down across his chest. He was breathing hard, his body rigid.

She looked up, right into his face. Their eyes locked. He reached out and cupped one of her breasts, his thumb gently abrading the tip.

She lurched and nearly fell on top of him, her hips meeting his.

"You're killing me," he said, his voice thick and choked. "I don't want to hurt you or scare you. I want this to be good for you." She could feel the evidence of his heavy arousal against her stomach, and she took a deep breath, wanting him so much she could barely concentrate.

"It's good for me," she said. "So very good. Seth?"

He simply looked at her, as if he couldn't speak.

"I don't want to wait," she said.

His chest rose and fell hard beneath her. He reached behind him for his pants and protection.

"Then we won't," he said, and he rolled her beneath him. Carefully he sheathed himself, his eyes never leaving hers. He gently trailed one finger from her lips to her throat to the tip of one breast.

She gasped, reached down and touched him, and then she opened for him. He surged beneath her hand and slid into her depths. He filled her.

Molly closed her eyes and moved with him, mindless, sightless, frantic. He started to withdraw and she cried out.

"Seth?"

"I'm here. I'm with you all the way. Stay with me."

And he moved with her, over and over again. She gazed into his eyes and stayed with him, every nerve in her body responding to him.

"Molly?"

"Yes." She breathed the word. "Yes, now. Don't wait. Please."

He didn't wait. Instead, he reached down and very lightly stroked her where their bodies met.

The world turned unbelievably bright. She cried out, and sunlight spilled over everything as her body answered his caress. Seth held her as the spasms passed, and then when she was almost still, almost past the pulsating bliss, he rocked into her again.

Once more she went over the edge as he threw back his head and went with her.

Long moments passed. Seth had turned on his side and tucked Molly against his chest. She moved in his arms.

"Stop that. I'm only human."

"Meaning you're tired?"

"Meaning I'm never going to be that tired. If you press against me, I'm bound to want to touch you."

But by now, she had wriggled around and was facing him. The streetlight had gone off and the very first hint of gray daylight was starting to filter into the shadowy room. Molly waited for her body to recover from the most exultant physical experience of her life. Seth had done something very special for her tonight. He had made her feel normal again. He had made her feel like a desirable woman, and he had done it, partly, by calling attention to his own scars in order to distract her from hers.

Even though he didn't like to talk about himself.

She reached out and gently traced the outline of the scar on his shoulder with her fingertip. "Ada told me that your family was lost in a fire."

He stiffened slightly, but he didn't pull away. "My parents. Neither Shannon nor I were in the house at the time. It started on the first floor with the dryer. I don't know why they didn't hear the smoke alarms, but the house was old and the flames caught quickly."

His voice cracked. Molly shook her head and touched his lips. "I shouldn't have asked. It's painful for you to talk about it."

But he kissed her fingertips. "We lived out in the country, pretty far from the nearest fire department. By the time I got there, though, there were two fire trucks in action. I was crazed. I charged past the firemen who were going in to try and get my parents out, but part of the ceiling collapsed on me. I was barely inside the door and they dragged me out. Then things started to cave. The coroner said that they died of smoke inhalation. They didn't suffer from the flames."

But that didn't matter, did it? Seth's voice was quiet, deathlike, as if he had perished in that house, too.

Fear gripped Molly. She looked into Seth's eyes and knew that he didn't really see her, as if he was lost with no way back.

Shannon, she thought. He always reacted when his sister came up. "Where was Shannon?" she asked.

He raised his head. "She was safe. At that point she was safe." And then his mask came down.

"Kiss me," he told her. "Let me make love with you again."

The subject of Shannon was closed. Molly looked into Seth's eyes, and all she saw was him. All she needed now was him.

Shannon could wait. Making love with Seth could not. And soon the bright light of morning would be here, their lives would separate again. She would step into her daytime world, he would retreat to his nighttime one. They wouldn't repeat this magic. Tonight was for one time only.

She slipped her arms around his neck. "Again," she whispered.

Chapter 17

It was a beat-up-on-yourself kind of day, Seth thought when he finally slammed back from his computer and gave up on writing anything. Not that he didn't beat up on himself regularly, but, hell, what the heck had he been thinking last night, making love with Molly?

"Thinking wasn't even a part of it," he said. "It was all physical, all heat and impulse." But he knew that he lied. She was starting to get to him.

"She got to you from day one," he admitted. Not that it mattered. Didn't change a thing. But one thing had to change. She would be coming home in a few hours and a few hours after that, he would be back at work. He couldn't watch her every minute and the alternative…letting her walk into that apartment every night alone?

Seth uttered a word he didn't use very often, not even on the street. Then he got up and left the house. He still had friends from the past. They didn't know much more about him than Ada or anyone else did, but they remained loyal when he let them.

One of them was a police officer who sometimes moonlighted as a security guard in his off-hours.

"Just the ticket," Seth said. Davis wouldn't let anything happen to Molly. She hadn't wanted him to report the home invasion to the police, but surely she could see the necessity of this.

That afternoon, when Molly got off from work, Seth was waiting outside the bakery. Her heart leapt at the sight of him, even as she berated herself. He was supposed to be sleeping right now; he had gotten barely any sleep last night.

"It's still light outside," she said. "Aren't you going to turn to dust or something?"

"Ah, a full day of hard labor and the woman can still give a man a hard time. I'm impressed, Molly." He fell into step beside her.

She chuckled. "I just—I wondered why you were here." Although she thought she knew. It wasn't because he couldn't wait to see her after they had made love last night. It was because of the break-in.

"I should have done this before," he told her.

"You have to sleep sometime."

"Sleep is low on my list of things I want to do right

now," and the dark tenor to his voice made her look up directly into his eyes. Her breath *whooshed* out of her body, and she wished they were back at her apartment already. Even though she wasn't going to make love to him again. It would be totally crazy and irresponsible to begin wanting this man on a regular basis. She couldn't really have him. She was on the run and might be on the run forever.

"But you're right," he was saying. "I can't be around twenty-four hours a day, so I've asked a friend to watch your place when I can't be there."

Molly glanced up and nearly stumbled. Ruthie was in an umbrella stroller Ada had found at a flea market, and the wheel caught on an uneven part of the sidewalk.

Seth caught them both.

"You've asked someone to...spy on me?"

"To look out for you."

"But he would be around watching me all the time."

"He would be looking out for your safety."

"Who?"

"His name is Arnie Davis. He's a police officer."

She thought she was going to be sick. "Seth, I can't."

They were nearing a park or what some people called a park. It was really just a small patch of grass surrounded by slabs of concrete covered in broken glass and cigarette butts. But there was a rickety bench there.

Seth drew her to it and helped her to sit down. Then he sat beside her and pulled Ruthie's stroller close so she could see Molly's face.

"Molly, he's a good man, a trustworthy man. And he can be there when I can't."

"Ruthie and I are okay on our own," she argued. Even though she didn't believe that one hundred percent, she couldn't get past the anxiety she felt every time she saw a police uniform. It had been Kevin's uniform that had first helped her to trust him. It was his abuse of that uniform that made her realize she didn't know enough about trust.

Seth could have told her that she was being unreasonable, she realized. He could have pointed to yesterday's break-in as proof that she and Ruthie weren't okay, but he didn't.

"I know what happened yesterday upset me, but that was because I was caught off guard. Today I'm fine."

Okay, that sounded like the lie that it was, but she couldn't put herself in the hands of a total stranger, a man whom she had never met. Especially not a police officer. She didn't know what had happened to Kevin. She hadn't heard a word, and the waiting, the not knowing was making her beyond jittery. She had come to Chicago because it was a huge city and she was looking for a place to disappear, but even a big city might not be safe. Was anyplace safe? If Seth had a friend in Chicago who was a police officer, Kevin might have *fifty* friends in Chicago who were police officers. And one of them might be Arnie Davis.

The only good thing about this was that at least—she hoped—Arnie Davis wouldn't hurt Seth. Still, that wasn't enough to induce her to risk Ruthie.

"I'm sorry," she said. "I've caused you so much trouble. I don't mean to cause you more."

"You need to be protected, Molly."

"I have to do it, Seth. I shouldn't have come to get you yesterday. I should have handled things."

"Like hell you should have." His eyes turned dark. He looked like some beautiful, damaged avenging angel.

"Seth…I appreciate everything you've done…so much, but I don't expect you to protect me. Maybe I don't even *want* you to protect me." Especially since she was getting him more and more tangled up with her. If Kevin found her and found out that someone had been shielding her…

"I know that," he said, his voice suddenly flat. "Molly, let Arnie guard you."

She shook her head. "I'm sorry. I know it would make things easier and you would worry less, but I just can't."

"Why?"

She looked away. What should she say? She took a deep breath. "I know it's stupid, but I'm afraid of police officers."

His stare was like a laser beam directed at her. "You're going to need to explain that."

She gave him an anguished look.

"Molly, who hurt you?" She was amazed that he didn't ask what she had done. It was what most people would do if someone announced they had a fear of policemen. But this was Seth. He was different, special. He lived by a different code.

"Seth," she whispered, "just take no for an answer, all right? This is something I can't talk about." If she did, he would try to help, and if he helped…

Seth suddenly looked at Ruthie. He swung his head back to Molly, a question in his eyes.

Molly quickly shook her head. "Ruthie isn't the product of rape, which is all I can say. I'm sorry I can't do as you ask, Seth."

"All right, then. I'll take you home." He didn't look happy.

"I need to go to Ada's."

"She's not there. When I told her I was taking you home, she told me to tell you she and Cecily were going to some book sale. Something about out-of-print magazines."

Molly nodded and they started off toward her house. When they arrived, there was a man outside leaning against a tree. Even had he not waved to Seth, Molly would have known he was the police officer. He seemed to take in everything in one swift glance; he was built like a linebacker. If she hadn't been so afraid that Kevin would eventually find a link to her through Arnie, she might have wanted the officer as a guard. But if one of Kevin's men found out an off-duty police officer was shielding her, it would just be too easy for him. And it would be all over for her and Ruthie.

Her door had been the only one in the building that

had been touched. What was that about? Simple breaking and entering? Maybe. Or maybe she'd been found.

"I'll be right back," Seth said, and he went over to talk to the man. There was a lot of gesturing, and Molly couldn't quite see, but she thought there was an exchange of money.

Seth came back and Arnie got into his car and drove off.

"Did you give that man money?"

Seth smiled at her tone. "Molly, he stood outside your house for an hour."

"Then I give him money." Even though she knew how many pennies exactly were in her purse, and there weren't many.

"Let me get this straight. You want me to let you pay for a bodyguard that I hired and that you didn't want."

"It was my house he was guarding."

"At my request."

"Doesn't matter." Seth was probably already wishing he had never found her on the sidewalk, without her costing him his hard-earned money. She started to reach for her purse.

"Let's get off the street," he said, and she was happy to do so. But once they got inside, she opened her purse.

"See, I learned one lesson. Never open your purse on the street."

He reached over her and snapped it shut. "I'm not taking your money. It's bad enough that you still insist on giving me that ten dollars a week, but this—for the record, Arnie wasn't going to let me pay him, either. He said you were too pretty and so was your baby." Which should have sounded good but didn't. It was Kevin's fervent hope that their baby would be a girl—and pretty enough for the cameras.

"Lock yourself in, Molly," Seth said. "And promise me you'll come get me if you need me."

"I will. Thank you."

He touched her cheek. "I'm sorry," he said.

"About what? You were doing a good thing."

"That's not what I'm sorry about." He ran his fingertips over her lips and let himself out the door. His footsteps stopped, until she turned the lock and then he moved off down the hall and out the building, the outside door falling shut with a thud behind him.

"What was he sorry for, Ruthie, do you think?" Maybe he was sorry she had turned away his offer of a bodyguard, or maybe he was sorry he had made love to her.

But she wasn't. Seth and Ada were the only good things to come out of this situation, and Seth's touch was a gift she would never have expected. It wasn't a gift he would give for good or that she could keep for long, but the memory would stay with her forever.

Not long afterward, Molly looked out the window and saw Seth sitting with his back against a tree. She opened the window. "Seth, please, you can't do this," she said.

"Watch me," he told her. "Or don't. I'd rather you went to sleep."

"What about you? You have to sleep sometime."

"I'll sleep in the morning. Now get some rest."

As if she would. All night she was going to dream of Seth. And there was nothing restful about remembering Seth's touch. If she was extremely fortunate, the sheets would not be smoldering come morning.

Seth dressed in his rags and headed for the streets when morning came. It was a time he rarely went out, and never to his usual haunts. His nighttime companions always scattered with the light to pursue their own activities, but he knew that if he asked around, he could find one or two of them, and what he had to say wouldn't wait.

Something was terribly wrong with Molly. First there had been that guy following her, then her apartment had been broken into. She had no discernible family or friends, no telephone, a mailbox with no name on it, and she had an unnatural fear of police officers. All that might be explained away. Perhaps it still could be, but Arnie had told Seth something yesterday that had changed everything. While Arnie was on watch, a brutish-looking man had been taking pictures of Molly's apartment building. What's more, the guy had been especially vigilant about taking a picture of the front door. He had even taken a photo of the numbers on the house. So two days in a row there had been suspicious activity around Molly's apartment.

Was she running from the law? Seth would have bet

his life she wasn't, which might simply mean that he was stupid, but he refused to believe otherwise. And—no matter the reason—the truth was that someone appeared to be interested in either Molly or her house. And she was a woman living in secrecy and fear. Someone might be after Molly.

"Well, they're not going to get her." He entered the library where he had heard Rip and Shuffle hung out. He found them over by the daily newspapers.

"Lightning?" Shuffle said.

His voice, even at a whisper, was noticeable in the stillness.

Seth motioned them outside. "I need to ask you a favor."

Both men looked taken aback. Nobody asked favors on the street. They were either offered or they weren't. Seth was changing the status quo.

But they followed him out to the sidewalk. "What's up?" Rip asked.

"I know this is unusual," Seth said, "but it's important. Very important. Are you willing to listen?"

"Of course."

"And I can trust you?"

Shuffle looked at Seth suspiciously. Rip fingered the brim of the hat that Seth had saved for him. "You can trust me," he said.

Which made Shuffle mad, so he agreed that he, too, could be trusted.

"All right," Seth said. "This is what I need you to do...."

* * *

That night as he sat on the street and took mental notes of what was happening, Seth wondered for the first time if he could ever be a different man. Would Molly have let him protect her if he hadn't been who he was?

Come on, he thought. She doesn't even know who you are. She doesn't just fear policemen, she dislikes reporters, remember?

She had let him touch her. No, more than that, she had asked him to touch her, and she had given every glorious inch of herself to him. Just thinking of her, he wanted to be beside her, on a feather bed this time, and he wanted to take it slow, to love her long and well.

But the word *love* made him close his eyes. Touching Molly had been more than a physical thing.

So don't do it again, he warned himself. She isn't for you. Love isn't for you. Don't let it happen. You might lose her, and you've already lost all that you can handle. You're not a whole person anymore. Half of you went missing years ago, and that means that when the initial glow ends, you'll surely end up hurting her. She's already been hurt by someone. We're talking major damage done here, McCabe.

And if he ever found out who had done that to her and what had caused her to end up alone and living in fear, heaven help the man. The streets would swallow him up.

And the streets didn't talk, not unless he wanted them to.

* * *

Last night had seemed as if it lasted forever, Molly thought as she made her way to Ada's the next evening. She had awakened several times and looked out to see that Seth had not left his post.

More than anything, she had wanted to go to him, to ask him to come inside with her, and that scared her to death. If there was ever anyone who was a loner, Seth was the one. He wanted her, but he didn't like it. He helped her—constantly—but that was because he had a streak of nobility he didn't even like to acknowledge. And while he looked at Ruthie with admiration, he also never got very close to her. Babies were obviously not his thing. A mother couldn't afford to get involved with such a man.

Her heart lurched, and she knew why. She was already falling for him. She closed her eyes against the painful truth.

When she opened them again, she looked straight into the lens of a camera. The man wielding it was across the street using a close-up lens.

Old memories attacked her. Reporters shoving microphones at her, yelling, asking questions she was too young to understand. Scaring her. Her parents punishing her if the stories were less than favorable. Cameras catching her smallest action. She was always alone, no friends, no anything.

Molly struggled against the panic that rushed in, harsh and suffocating and disabling. She wanted to scream at the cameraman, to yank the camera from his grasp, to crush it on the sidewalk. But she had Ruthie with her.

"What are you doing?" she heard herself asking. "Who are you? What do you want? I see you. I know your face. I'll remember it. Give me that camera."

For a second, the man froze. Then he pivoted and dashed away.

Molly stood there shivering, trying to think, to breathe.

"Ma'am, are you all right?" a soft voice asked.

She looked up and saw a scarecrowlike man standing ten feet away from her. He was wearing torn clothing and obviously hadn't had a bath too recently, but there was concern on his face.

Quickly she nodded. "Thank you, yes, I'm fine." And then she rushed down the last block to Ada's and let herself into the sanctuary of the old brick building.

"It was one of Kevin's hirelings," she whispered to herself, and she knew she was right. This was not a part of town tourists frequented, and there was no reason in the world for anyone to be taking pictures of her. Unless they needed to supply proof that she had been spotted.

It was almost time to run again, she thought. But her next thought was a silent cry.

Seth. She would have to leave him.

"But when we do, Ruthie, we're going to make an attempt to make sure he isn't alone." Right or wrong, she wanted to do something good for Seth, and the only thing she could think of that would have any meaning for him involved Shannon.

For that she would need information...and help. Molly knocked on Ada's door and waited.

Chapter 18

"Ada, I need your help," Molly began when Ada had opened the door.

"Oh, hon, of course I'll watch Ruthie. That's what you want, isn't it?" Ada's voice was soft and creaky. She looked at Ruthie with absolute adoration, and for a minute Molly felt ashamed. Ada had become almost a mother to her, a grandmother to Ruthie. Now that things were ending, she wondered if she had really ever taken the time to thank her properly.

"You're a truly good friend," Molly said, tears gathering behind her eyes. "What would I have done without you these past weeks?" She stepped forward and hugged the older woman.

Ada went stiff. For several seconds, she just patted

Molly's back awkwardly and then she hugged her back tightly. "Well, heck, hon, who wouldn't want to help you and Ruthie? I may be cranky, but I'm not stupid."

"No," Molly agreed with a trembling smile as she and Ada moved apart. "You are certainly never stupid. You've got more street smarts than almost anyone I know."

"Well, yes, I guess I do," Ada said, puffing out her chest. "Now, do you want me to keep that baby or not?"

"Yes, but not yet. That's not the help I need. I need to know about Shannon."

"Oh, hon, not that," Ada reprimanded.

"Yes, that. He won't say it, but he misses her. There must be something someone can do."

"Not a thing. I've tried. He doesn't want to talk about it."

"I know, but I've met her," Molly admitted.

Ada raised her brows. "She talked to you?"

"Uh-huh, although she didn't want to. She was following Seth. That has to mean something good."

"Maybe it just means she's a no-good sneak." Although Ada's tone implied she thought otherwise.

Molly frowned. "She seemed to really care about him."

"That's the tragedy of it, isn't it? Every time he sends her a check and she sends it back, it tears him up inside. They've both had hard lives and, I'm guessing, a lot of past to live down. How can you go back and change the past?"

Molly wished there was an answer to that. "Ada, will you help me?"

Ada's eyes were troubled. "Honey, just leave it alone. I'd like to help Seth, too, but what you're talking about—he won't thank you for it. Seth has secrets, and he wants it that way. I've tried to talk him into going to see his sister, to attempt to start fresh, but they're both too wounded, I guess. There are things you and I don't know about, and some things have to be left alone. They can't be fixed."

Molly sighed. "Maybe you're right." She took Ruthie out of her carrier and cuddled her close. She'd kept her daughter biding her time for long minutes, but immediately Ruthie snuggled up to her. How nice to be able to fix things easily, with a little cuddling.

Sitting in the nearest chair, Molly glanced down, noticing for the first time the many stacks of magazines lying around the room.

"Cecily and I went shopping to the used bookstores. We just love old movies," Ada explained.

But Molly was suddenly suffocating. There, lying almost at her feet, was her own childhood image staring back at her. Quickly she rose. She looked at Ada, trying to think of something light to say, some way to get rid of that magazine, to get out of this situation. For Ruthie's sake, she was fully prepared to lie, even though she hated lying to a friend.

Still, when she looked up, she realized that it was too late to lie or run or stall. Ada was staring at the magazine's cover, too.

"For the love of Lake Michigan, how could I have missed that?" Ada asked. "Cecily sorted these, but still, I've been wondering who you were for weeks. It *is* you, isn't it? Little Molly Marsh, the Sweet Stuff fruit juice girl," she said, using the too-cute name the agency had used for some of the commercials Molly had done. "Of course, it's you. Who else has that smile?"

Molly stood frozen. She felt as if all the blood had drained from her body, and she swallowed hard as Ada looked up and stared straight into her face. "Don't tell," she managed to whisper. "Promise me you won't tell anyone, Ada. It's important."

Ada gazed at her for long moments. Molly swayed slightly on her feet, clutching Ruthie protectively.

"I don't understand, but if it's important," Ada finally said, "then it's important. And, as I've told you before, I don't rat on my friends. You all right?"

A tear ran down Molly's cheek.

Ada swore. "Don't look like that, now. I said I wouldn't tell."

Molly swiped at the tear. "It's not that, at least it's not that I'm afraid you'll tell. I trust your word. That's why I'm crying, I guess. It's been such a long time since I could trust anyone."

"Well," Ada said, pulling herself up tall. "I don't know what's happened to you, but things are different now. You've got me and Seth. You've got friends."

"I know," Molly said. "How lucky I was to fall where I did that day. Thank you, Ada." And Ada, her eyes filled with concern, endured yet another hug from Molly.

But when Molly left not long after that, she knew that she wouldn't have her friends much longer. Kevin was coming, and she couldn't put Ada and Seth in danger. She had to get out with a lot of noise and bluster so that he would know she had gone and he wouldn't bother interrogating anyone who had known her in Chicago.

"Would you like me to go now?" Seth asked, coming up behind Molly and kneading her shoulders. She had been tense and nervous all evening, not paying as much attention to her lessons as she usually did. "You probably need some rest." He bent his head and kissed the side of her neck.

She leaned into his touch, reaching up to place her palm on his face.

"I don't want you to go. You'll only go sit outside, anyway. I can't sleep when you're out there."

"Why? Do I make you nervous?" His voice was rough. "That was never my intent."

"I know." She turned in his arms and faced him. "And no, you don't make me nervous. It's just that when you're that close but not actually here with me, I miss you."

Her last words were barely a whisper. He had to lean close to hear them, but when he did, something deep and possessive and purely male filled his soul. "You make me do the most irrational things," he said, and pulled her hard against him. "You know I should be outside watching the street."

"The street isn't going anywhere, and no one is going to hurt me while you're here with me." She rose on her toes and kissed his jaw.

He growled. "You're damn right about that. Still…"

"I need you here tonight," she said. "Just for tonight." And she looped an arm around his neck and leaned against him, her breasts brushing against his chest.

"Molly?"

"Yes, Seth?"

"I only have so much self-control."

She touched her lips to his and smiled slightly. "You have too much self-control." And leaning back in his arms, she placed her fingers where her lips had been just seconds earlier. "You also have the most amazing mouth. Touch me with your mouth tonight, Seth. Tomorrow you can sit outside if you want to."

As if he wanted to be outside when she was here inside. But he was too near the edge to talk. Instead, he wound his fingers in her hair and covered her mouth with his own. He indulged himself with long, hard, hot, wet kisses. He lapped at the hollow of her throat, his fingers quickly unfastening her buttons and freeing her breasts, so that he could taste them, too.

She arched against him, her breath kicking up high. "Seth?"

"Shh, I'm feasting," he told her, and then his lips

closed around her turgid nipple. Her hips jerked against his, and he lowered her to the carpeted floor.

Slicking her jeans and her panties down her legs and removing his own clothing, he took everything away, until she was naked beneath him, and then he kissed her belly and the tantalizing triangle of curls that hid her from him.

He looked up then, from where he was kneeling next to her. She was gazing directly into his eyes. "I should kiss you, too," she said.

Seth gave her a slow smile. "You will, next time. This is my turn." And he parted her legs, knelt between them and lifted her for his kiss. He made it slow, covering her fully.

Molly cried out. She writhed, and then she convulsed against his mouth. A deep sense of satisfaction laced with need for her filled him, but he ignored his need. He held her, never leaving her, letting her come down slowly.

Then he kissed her again…and again. She went wild. He closed his eyes and considered himself blessed to be able to touch her this way.

When he finally released her, she was almost sobbing, but when he started to lie down with his hand beneath her neck, she shook her head.

"Oh, no," she said. "You promised I'd get a turn." And she rose to her knees, placed one hand on his chest and pushed gently, urging him back onto the rug. "I believe in fair play," she said, kissing his mouth and then his chest, pausing at his nipples.

He barely held back a gasp, and he felt her smile against his skin. "Who said this was fair?" He choked the words out.

But she was already continuing down along the flat plane of his stomach, over his abdomen. She found what she was seeking and kissed him there, too. He shuddered and struggled for control.

She kissed him again. Her fingers were like fluttering butterflies caressing him, making him completely, totally insane. His body was aflame for her. He had to have her now, right now.

Reaching down, his hands spanned her waist.

"Seth," she protested, but then he lifted her onto him. He impaled her, and she slid down the length of him.

"Seth," she drawled. "Yes, Seth." She found her rhythm, bracing her hands on his chest. He tried to hold back, but she wouldn't let him. He was never going to be able to wait.

With a supreme effort, he reached down and touched her where their bodies joined. Her body tensed. She cried out, and as the waves of her orgasm tightened her muscles around him, he went with her, the world falling away.

"Yes, Molly," he finally managed to say in a ragged, shaky voice. He pulled her into his arms and tucked her in beside him, dragging a comforter off the couch to cover her.

Then, he must have slept, because when he looked over at her next, she was staring into his eyes, the moonlight hitting her full in the face.

Such a beautiful face and so sad. "Molly, I'm sorry if I was too rough. Did I hurt you?"

She shook her head, and then she leaned over and kissed him. "You couldn't." But there was such distress in her voice, such resignation.

Gently she moved back into his arms. They made love again, but the sadness never really left her eyes. She seemed distant, resigned. Fear slithered through him. If this wasn't a prelude to a goodbye scene, he didn't know what was. She had dropped into his life and now, he would swear she was thinking about dropping out again.

How could he protect her if she wasn't here? He didn't even go near the question of what he was going to do with his life when she wasn't in it anymore.

Seth didn't know a thing, except this: if she was going, he was going to have to make sure she was safe. Tomorrow he would check in with Rip and Shuffle and see if they had seen anything suspicious. It would mean another daylight run, more questionable behavior and a greater chance of blowing his cover.

Who cared, he thought as he kissed Molly's temple and watched her as she finally gave in to exhaustion. He would risk a lot to make sure she stayed free and safe. If she was better off elsewhere, so be it.

Today was the day, Molly told herself as she rushed down the street after having delivered some of Ada's chicken soup to an ailing Cecily. It was the least she could do for Ada, Molly thought, and it gave Ada one last chance to baby-sit Ruthie. Because this was it. Her last full day in town. Tomorrow she would tell Mr. Alex she was leaving. Then she would make a lot of noise and bluster about packing and getting herself out of her apartment. It hurt her to think that she wouldn't be telling Ada or Seth goodbye, but if she let them know that she was leaving, they would only worry, maybe even try to stop her.

And this way they wouldn't have to lie to anyone about not knowing anything about when and where she had gone.

"I'm not sure where I am going, anyway," she muttered. St. Louis or Milwaukee would be logical next stops but probably too obvious. Maybe she should keep moving for a while, the farther away from here the better.

Something sharp stabbed at her heart. She would never be coming back here again. Probably a good thing. She was in love with Seth, and having someone like her loving him couldn't do him any good. She had too much baggage. Her whole life would be lived looking over her shoulder.

As if her life had become a movie, Molly suddenly got a creepy feeling, the hair on the back of her neck standing up. Soft footsteps sounded behind her. She stopped and so did the footsteps. Schooling herself not to panic or to let it show that she was aware of the person, Molly slowly began to put the brakes on her pace.

She looked in the closed-shop windows, pretending interest she didn't feel while listening, staying constantly aware of any movement behind her. She pretended to amble, to be unaware of her stalker. She feigned normalcy. Finally she reached the area she was looking for and entered an open drugstore.

At last she was out of sight of her pursuer. Her legs felt like soggy noodles, but she kept breathing, forcing herself to examine a spinner rack of magazines near the window. Flipping through a magazine and keeping her eyes straight ahead, she glanced out the corner of her eye to the street. Nothing.

Fear gripped her. Of course, maybe the person following her hadn't been following her at all.

I'm starting to see monsters where they don't exist, she told herself, but she still couldn't force herself to leave the bright lights and safety of the store. She continued to stare sightlessly at the magazine.

And then, out of the corner of her eye, she saw the merest hint of a flip of blond hair, a slight body, a woman who gave her a quick perusal, shook her head and turned to go.

Shannon. In a flash, Molly was to the door.

Carefully she opened it, trying not to make any noise. If Shannon knew she was now the one being followed, she might pick up the pace, and there was a good chance Shannon could run faster than she could.

So she bided her time. She stayed far behind in the shadows, using the information Ada and Seth had given

her, only in reverse this time. If Shannon stopped, she
stepped back and stopped, too. If she hadn't been so
heartbroken and worried and guilty about what she was
doing, nosing into Seth's business when she hated anyone nosing into hers, this might have been fun.

It seemed as if they walked for miles, although Molly
couldn't really have said for sure. All of her attention
was on Shannon.

Finally Shannon halted in front of an apartment
building. "So, are you coming, or not?" she called, turning to look in Molly's direction.

Molly blinked, but she didn't back off. "I'm coming." She closed the last half block that remained between them. "How long did you know I was there?"

Shannon shrugged. "All the way from the drugstore."

"So why didn't you leave me in the dust or tell me
to get lost?"

Frowning, Shannon shook her head. "I want some
answers. If you were going to come to me, why should
I argue?"

"I want some answers, too."

Shannon's brows knit together. "We'll see."

"One thing I want to know is why you keep spying on
your brother," Molly said as if Shannon hadn't even spoken. "You won't talk to him, but you follow him around."

"That's my business."

"It's *my* business when I'm the one being followed.
Do you hate Seth so much that you won't even show
your face to him?"

Shannon shoved open the door and went inside, her shoulders hunched and tense. "You comin'?" she asked. "Because if you are, close the door behind you."

Molly followed her inside the building and into her apartment. When they were safely inside, Shannon whirled, "Listen, lady, don't go telling me how I feel or don't feel about my own brother. You don't know a thing."

Leaning against the closed door, Molly studied the tense woman. "You're right, I don't. But I care about Seth's happiness, and I know that he has ghosts that haunt him. I'll bet you know why. Surely there's some way to help him."

"Don't bother trying to change the past. It's done."

"I know that. I have my own past. It's not the past I want to change, but I don't think Seth can be truly happy if he doesn't leave it behind. Forgive me, but...do you care at all about him?"

Shannon took a step toward Molly. "I should probably scratch your eyes out." She waited.

So did Molly.

Finally Shannon groaned. "All right, you think you can find some way to make him happy, maybe you're right. I know he's spent the last couple of nights at your place. If you can make a difference, maybe telling you will be worth it." She walked to a faded green couch and sat down.

Molly followed her.

Shannon looked away. "I was only fourteen when

our parents died in a fire. Seth never said so, but I know he blamed himself for their deaths. He thought that if he had been there earlier he might have saved them."

She gave a short, harsh laugh. "I don't know. He probably would have died, too, and it wasn't his fault he wasn't home when the fire began, but for a long time, I hated him for living when they died. I let him know it, too. I'm sure it hurt him, but at the time, well, I didn't care." She looked up. "Don't look at me that way."

"What way?" Molly asked.

"As if you feel sorry for me."

Molly dragged in a breath. "Don't *you* feel sorry for you? You lost your parents and you pushed away the only person you had left. It's understandable, but still sad. To have a brother…" she began, but then she stopped. "Go on. Tell me what happened between now and then."

"Lots of things I don't want to remember. Seth was strict, and I didn't like that. I argued with him all the time. I told him I hated him. When I was almost eighteen I ran away to San Francisco. For just over a year I lived on the street. I was scared, I was lost, but I couldn't go home."

"Why not?"

Shannon pulled at a loose thread on the old couch. "No money. Too much pride. I figured Seth would lock me up and never let me out of the house again, and then…there was this guy. I…did things for him, stuff I don't like to think about, bad stuff. He terrified me. I was afraid of running from him and afraid he would hurt Seth if I called him." Her voice broke slightly and Molly fought to keep herself seated, the urge to comfort Shannon was so great. She wanted to tell her that she knew just what she meant about being afraid of a man and about fearing for Seth's safety as a result, but she couldn't do that.

"One day Blix, the guy I told you about, found out I was pregnant. He beat me until I was half-dead. I didn't know what I was doing. Somehow I got out of there and onto the street. For days I lived in filth, running whenever I thought Blix might be near. That was how Seth found me, lying in an alley in a pile of rags covered in blood from the miscarriage I'd had. He took me home, he found me this place, a job, and then I sent him away. That's it, that's all."

"I don't understand." Molly couldn't keep the concern from her voice.

"No, you couldn't," Shannon told her. "For years I'd thrown everything he'd tried to do for me right back in his face and then I ran away and became all the things I knew he'd hate most. I needed to make myself clean, to make amends, but there wasn't any way to do that. I couldn't continue to be his sister and live with what I had done to him and what I had become, so I took the hand up he gave me and then I set him free."

"But he isn't free."

"I know that," Shannon said with a cry, "but don't

you understand? Seth saw himself as my parent, my protector. He's the man who blamed himself for our parents' death. How much do you think he blames himself for what happened to me on the streets? Every time he looks at me, he beats himself up and it never stops, because irreparable things happened to me while I was gone. So let me watch over him from a distance now and then, and leave the rest alone. You can't make this better. You can't wish the past away."

Molly stared at Shannon's stricken expression and felt her own heart breaking for all that had happened to Seth and his sister. She thought of her own parents and their betrayal, her betrayal at Kevin's hands, her mistakes.

"You can't wish the past away," she agreed quietly. "I know about that. I have a lot of experience with it."

"So you can go back home now."

Closing her eyes for a second, Molly tried to think of the right words. "I don't like to think about my past, but it's only the future that concerns me these days. Seth needs a future."

"With you?"

Molly shook her head. "That's not possible, but he could still have a future with his sister. Start from now, don't talk about what already happened. He worries about you. I can tell."

Shannon studied her for a long time. "I don't want to hurt him anymore, and I'm sure I would. I'm not an easy person to put up with. It's better that Seth and I maintain some distance between us."

Molly opened her mouth to speak.

"No," Shannon told her.

"You're sure? That's absolutely final?"

"I'm absolutely certain, but how about you? What *is* going on between you and Seth? And don't tell me nothing is happening. I allowed you in here today, I talked to you today because I know he does mean something to you, so don't try to lie to me. It wouldn't do you any good."

"I suppose it wouldn't," Molly agreed, "but what's going on between Seth and myself isn't permanent. I'm leaving town soon, I won't be bothering you again, and you won't have to worry that I'll hurt your brother. I would never willingly do that."

"What about unwillingly?"

Molly's heart skipped a beat, just because that was the same fear she had had several times now. Had she put Seth in danger by letting him get close?

"I'll do anything I can to make sure nothing bad happens to Seth." She rose to leave and made her way to the door.

Shannon got up, too. "You weren't that terrible at tailing me. Was that Seth who taught you?"

"Yes."

Shannon nodded. "Tell him...no, don't tell him anything. Don't tell him you were here."

Molly nodded her agreement and moved out of the apartment quickly. Ada was probably already worrying.

Pushing through the building's front door, her shoulder was suddenly shoved back. A loud clatter and several thumps ensued as something hit the ground and two feet shot out and tangled with her own. Molly fell to the door's threshold, caught between the door and whoever was outside.

"Double damn it to hell," a deep male voice said.

Molly's heart started trotting triple time as she struggled to get to her feet and run.

"What in the universe is going on here?" Shannon's voice raged as she came rushing out of the hall, leapt over Molly, shoved back the door and threw herself on the man trying to rise. "You again!" she said.

"Again?" Molly asked weakly. "You know him? Who is he?"

"He's a low-down scum-sucking sneak, that's who," Shannon declared. "Don't lie to me again. Who exactly are you and what is it that you want?" She glanced down at the ground where a camera lay shattered. "You were taking pictures?" She dropped to her knees and pummeled the man.

"Shannon, look out," Molly warned. The guy was a big man. He could easily have subdued Seth's petite sister. Instead, he let her beat at him, only holding out his hands to fend off the worst of her punches. Finally Shannon realized he wasn't lashing out at her and she stopped.

"Well?" she asked, her hands on her hips.

He sat up, leaning on both elbows. "I'm Jeff Payton of the *Chicago Sentinel*."

"A reporter?" Molly's voice was weak. She suddenly felt sick as she finished scrambling to her feet.

Jeff slowly rose. He gave her a nod. "Yes, ma'am."

"Why…why are you following *us?*" she managed to ask. She had to know.

"I'm not. Exactly. It's Seth McCabe I'm interested in. Both of you ladies seem to have a connection to him." Molly noticed that while he nodded at her, his gaze lingered on Shannon.

"So what?" Shannon asked. "And why would you want to do a story on Seth?"

"You don't know what he does for a living?" Jeff raised one incredulous eyebrow.

Shannon, amazingly enough, blushed. "If you've been following me, then you know Seth and I don't talk often." Molly applauded her for the lie. Why tell a reporter that they didn't talk at all?

But the man gave Shannon an amused and appreciative glance. "You are an amazing and brazen woman," he said. "I like that."

Shannon glared at him.

"You still haven't answered the question," Molly told Jeff. She refused to ask questions about Seth. She wouldn't pry any more than she had, especially not with a reporter trying to do a story on him, but she needed to know if this man meant him harm.

"I've been following Mr. McCabe for weeks. I have strong reasons to believe that he is Nick Dawson who writes the 'Mean Streets' column for the *Chicago Standard.*"

Molly thought she was going to be sick. She caught

at the door frame to keep herself from falling. "Seth is a reporter?"

"The best."

Molly's world was suddenly whirling, shaking to pieces. She had told Seth she hated reporters…several times. Yet, he had never said a thing, never revealed himself. Why? She clutched at her stomach.

But Shannon turned a suspicious look on Jeff Payton. "So why are you tailing Seth if he works for a rival newspaper?"

"I planned to do a story on him."

"You jerk," Shannon yelled. "You know the guy that writes that column risks his life every night. And you're going to blow his cover?" She practically shrieked the words.

Jeff held up both hands. "I said that I *planned* to do a story. No more. It wouldn't be right. I've been following him—and you—for too long now. I've learned what he's like, and I've got too much respect for him to out him now."

"You'd give up a story?" Molly was incredulous.

"I'll find another story," he said with a sigh. He looked genuinely chagrined, but could they actually trust him to be telling the truth? She'd known plenty of unscrupulous reporters who had been willing to lie to get her to talk to them.

"So, if you're not planning on doing an article on my brother anymore, then why are you still following us around?" Shannon asked.

"Well, that's another story completely," Jeff said with a slow smile. "I discovered a few things I hadn't expected to."

Molly noticed that he was looking at Shannon as if she had just turned into a goddess. So, okay, maybe he did have interests outside of getting a byline in a major newspaper.

"What kinds of things did you discover?" Shannon asked.

"Good things," Jeff assured her.

"How does she know you're really a reporter for the *Chicago Sentinel?*" Molly asked suddenly, seeing all too clearly which way the wind was blowing.

He pulled out his press pass and tossed it to her.

"Could be fake," she said.

"Call the *Sentinel,*" he offered. To Molly's surprise, Shannon went inside and did just that.

"He's actually real," she said, blinking with consternation. "So what are the things you discovered?" she asked again.

Jeff gave Molly a look that told her he didn't want to say what he had to say to a third party.

"Shannon, I need to go home now, but I don't want to leave you alone with this guy."

"Don't worry, I talked to my landlady. She's looking out the window and she's holding her phone at the ready. And anyway, if he does anything funny, I'll just kick him in the head. I've taken a few self-defense courses these past few years."

Molly nodded. "Don't tell him anything important, though," she warned Shannon.

Shannon gave her a look that implied she hadn't gone crazy yet and Molly left, headed back toward Ada's.

All the way down the streets all she could hear were Jeff Payton's words: Seth McCabe is a reporter, Seth McCabe is a reporter.

Her heart physically hurt. She wanted nothing more than to fall to her knees and sob, but crying had never gotten her anywhere.

Molly put one foot in front of the other. She turned another corner.

And that was when someone stepped out of a doorway, grabbed her from behind and pinioned her arms.

Chapter 19

Molly twisted and turned. She made her body go limp, dropping her center of gravity so that the person holding her lost his grip on her and she could kick out with her feet. She screamed *Fire* at the top of her lungs and scooted back, kicking out when the heavy-lidded thug came near her.

"For Christ's sake, Dom, get her under control. Grab her," another voice called, and Dom came toward her, red-faced and with murder in his eyes.

Molly thought she was going to faint. This man was going to kill her if she didn't get out of here. She threw her head back and screamed again, lashing out and kicking Dom in the groin.

He went down with a thud in a stream of unintelligible swear words, threats and groans as he clutched his injured parts.

"Hit her," he finally eked out. "Get her. Do it. Now."

More arms grabbed her. A piece of cloth was stuffed into her mouth. She tried to twist, and what she saw made her blood freeze. Besides Dom, there were four other men, not one of whom looked as if he had an ounce of mercy in his body.

She was going to die on the street. She would never see Ruthie or Seth again.

Seth was working when his phone rang.

"Mr. McCabe?" a man's voice said. "My name is Rip."

Seth was instantly alert. "Yes."

"I was told to call you if I saw anything funny going on with a woman named Molly Delavan. Well, I saw something. It don't look right."   •

He told Seth what he had seen. A bit hesitantly, he admitted that he had sent Shuffle in to pick the man's pocket. They had a wallet, some names, maybe some phone numbers.

Seth took the information down. He was typing into his computer, calling up information even as he spoke to Rip. "Meet me at the corner by Vince's Barbershop," he told Rip.

"Meet you?" Rip sounded confused. "Nobody said nothing about meeting anyone."

Seth closed his eyes. He took a deep breath. "Rip, an innocent woman's life may be in danger."

Rip swore. "I knew that guy with the camera looked bad. Oh, well, in that case, if it's that woman, we have to help. She's nice. She's got a baby. I've seen them both, so heck, yes, we'll be there. How will I know you?"

"You'll know me, I promise. Just look for Lightning."

And he hung up the phone.

Molly stared at the men gathered in front of her. They looked like animals, salivating just before the kill.

"Can we touch her?" one of them asked.

"Mr. Rickman only said to catch her," Dom said, but there was murder in his eyes. "Of course, Mr. Rickman's on his way, but he ain't here right now." He smiled.

Molly fought the nausea that threatened to disable her. She was choking on the dirty cloth in her mouth. She was being held with her arms behind her back. But as the first man came toward her, she kicked out fiercely, trying to throw her body forward.

The man slid away. She let all of her weight fall and the man holding her dropped her.

"What the hell? Get her!"

She kicked again, blindly, and caught skin and bone.

"Damn whore. Forget Rickman. I'm killing her now."

Desperate, she feinted and kicked again. Dom advanced on her, but he paused as a car door slammed and footsteps sounded behind Molly. Then a big hand clamped down on her foot, and she tumbled to the pavement. She kicked more, trying to release herself, her hair falling in her face. Savagely she pushed it aside, looking up to better assess her assailant. And found herself staring straight into the glassy blue eyes of Kevin Rickman.

He gave her a slow, greasy smile. "Miss me, Molly, my love? It's been a long time, hasn't it?"

Her heart had been beating frantically before. Now it thudded harder, practically rattling out of her body. Kevin released her foot. He reached out and grasped her by the throat, squeezing a bit.

She scratched him, and he swore, slapping her hard.

"I could cut her for you right now if you want," Dom said. "Slit her from ear to ear." Dom looked as if he was itching to do just that. After the blow she had given him he was still pasty-faced and limping.

"Oh, but then she wouldn't be pretty, would she, Dom? She's of no use to me unless she's pretty." He gave Molly a sickeningly confident wink.

She struggled to breathe through her fear and the cloth that was choking her. How had she gotten involved with this man? It could only have been her grief and need, after her aunt's death had left her alone. But reasons didn't matter now, did they? Think, Molly, think, she told herself. What would Seth have you do? What would Shannon do?

And slowly, though fear still ran through her, she ordered her body to calm. She took a big mental step back from her situation and looked closely at the man who held her fate in his hands. Kevin was physically strong—he worked out—and he had all these beefy men working for him, too. But he was not a man, really, not like Seth was. Next to Seth he was small in spirit, devoid of human caring, no man at all. Just a cruel insect. Shannon would have spit in his eye.

Forcing herself to remain steady, to ignore the nearly overwhelming urge to scream or struggle, Molly climbed to her feet. She steeled herself to look directly into Kevin's soulless eyes.

"You want to talk like a reasonable person now?" he asked. "No more screaming or trying to kick Dom in the nuts?"

She gave a slow nod, and Kevin reached out, flicking the cloth from her mouth. Slowly she worked her jaw, trying to make sure she could swallow and breathe and talk clearly. Then she looked up at Kevin.

"You scum-sucking snake," she said, stealing some of Shannon's words. "You may have me in your grip now, but I will see you in hell before I let you keep me, Rickman. I'll never stay with you. You disgust me." She started to bring her knee up again, but someone behind her grabbed her arms and pulled her back, dragging her across the pavement.

Kevin threw back his head and laughed. "Oh, this is good. I like this. The innocent little milkmaid turned tough girl. That's even better than I hoped for. It'll definitely attract the kind of attention I want."

"Will kidnapping attract the kind of attention you want?"

"What kidnapping, Molly? I came to see my daughter, and you are the mother of my daughter. Not a very fit mother, either, judging by the digs you've been living in. Consorting with street scum, dragging your daughter through dangerous streets after dark. I'm sure if a judge had to choose between you and a man of the law, well…" He held out his hands in dismissal.

She fought back the nausea his words brought on, but she refused to let him see how much he was scaring her.

With a snap of his fingers, he signaled one of the men behind her, and a thick piece of dark cloth covered her eyes. Someone tied her hands behind her back. "Phase one completed," Kevin said.

Molly's heartbeat started to gallop harder. Phase one meant there was a phase two, and that inevitably concerned her child.

Stay calm, she told herself. Listen for clues to where you're going, stay alert, look for opportunities to get away and get to Ruthie.

Seth will find us ran through her head, but she knew that was just wishful thinking. Seth didn't have a clue that she had been kidnapped. She was on her own.

"Come this way, Molly," Kevin said. "You've caused me a lot of trouble and cost me a lot of money. I don't like losing money." He gave her a hard push in the direction he wanted her to go.

She stumbled slightly and nearly went to her knees,

but she caught herself in time to stay on her feet. She took one step.

The night erupted in an earsplitting cacophony of cries and howls. Bodies rushed past her.

"What the hell?" Kevin yelled just near her elbow. Instinctively, she turned and kicked out, aiming high. Kevin let out a muffled "oof." She heard the scrape of his feet as he staggered, but she knew she hadn't gotten in a proper blow.

He let out a string of foulmouthed curses, including just what he intended to do to her. Completely disoriented, she tried to move aside but knew the blow was coming soon and blindfolded and tied up as she was, she would not be able to sidestep it.

And then she heard a sickening thud, a guttural sound coming out of a man's throat. Hands fumbled at her head.

She tried to move away.

"Now, miss, hold still, will ya, or I can't get this thing off." And suddenly she could see, the blindfold gone.

Molly stared straight into the face of a grizzled man wearing tattered clothing. He gave her a deep bow. "Rip at your service, ma'am." He reached behind her and released the bonds that held her hands.

She blinked and rubbed her wrists. "Thank you, Rip," she managed to say. "I've seen you somewhere."

"On the street near your house. Lightning sent me to watch over you."

"Lightning?" She became increasingly aware of the sound of fists smacking against flesh, of men struggling to defeat other men. Rip gestured around him.

Several other men who were dressed a lot like Rip were mixing it up with Kevin's thugs, two or three of Rip's friends to one of Kevin's.

"No sense in fighting fair with a bunch who would kidnap a woman," Rip explained.

"I...thank you," she said again, "but who's Lightning?"

Rip pointed behind her.

She turned and saw Seth's police officer friend battling with Dom.

"That's Lightning?" she asked.

"No, down there by the fire hydrant."

And then she looked halfway down the street. Seth faced Kevin head-on. There was thunder in Seth's expression, but Kevin's was cold, bloodless, evil. And then Kevin jabbed out quickly with something he held in one hand, hitting Seth square on the jaw.

Molly cried out as Seth staggered back. She would have run down the street if Rip hadn't grabbed her arm.

"No, you don't want to interrupt, ma'am, not with two that look like that. But don't worry. I've seen Lightning take a knife nick from a man the size of Paul Bunyan and come out the winner."

Maybe, she thought, but Kevin wasn't completely sane, she didn't think. He was fit and he was reckless and determined. And money was at stake. He took another hard swing at Seth, clipping him enough to send Seth spinning.

"Oh, you don't like me, do you?" Kevin snarled. "Well, how about this? I had her in my bed before you even knew she existed. I'll have her again. A thousand times, whenever I want her."

Nausea slid through Molly. She wanted to run to Seth and tell him that Kevin was nothing compared to him, but Rip was jumping up and down.

"Uh-oh," he said. "That wasn't smart at all."

She had half a second to wonder what he meant before Seth's fist came up and plunged into Kevin's stomach. One blow, two, three in rapid succession. Kevin staggered backward across the street, Seth following him all the way, his superior height making him tower over Kevin's shorter more heavily muscled body.

"Touch her again, ever, and I'll feast on your bones," Seth said, before he threw another short series of punches, sending Kevin crashing to the ground.

Kevin lay there, breathing hard, but then he spoke. "The baby's mine," he said.

"Not anymore," Seth told him. "She's Molly's and only Molly's."

"I have the DNA to prove it. What's more, I'm a cop, you're obviously street scum. Who do you think the authorities will believe, especially since I have friends in legal circles." He started to get up. Seth hit him again, in the face this time.

Kevin spit out a tooth and fell back to the ground.

"Ah well, I guess that's it, then," Seth said, rubbing his bloodied knuckles and staring down at Kevin. "I know who you are. One of my friends passed on some information and I looked you up. You do, indeed, have friends in legal circles. That gives you the power, doesn't it? Or maybe not. Those friends might not want to have anything to do with you after today, especially since two of *my* friends here are off-duty policemen who witnessed the kidnapping of an innocent civilian by a man who once took an oath to serve and protect. They're more than willing to talk to your friends in legal circles and tell them everything they know about you. You're worse than a criminal, because you're a criminal cop and there are plenty of witnesses here who'll testify to that."

Kevin let out a string of four-letter words.

"Maybe if you're really lucky, you won't get too much time in prison, but I doubt it," Seth told him, and then he signaled to his friends, who gave Molly a quick nod and then moved in to cuff Kevin and his friends. A squad car could already be heard roaring down the street.

"She'll need to come in to the station, Seth," one of the officers said.

"Tomorrow," Seth said.

The man nodded.

"Thank you," Molly called out, including all the men surrounding her. "Thank you all."

"It was worth it, ma'am. I haven't had this much fun

in years," one man said. And then he ducked his head. "Shuffle's the name," he told her.

She smiled at him and reached out her hand.

He looked as if she had offered to do something horrifying.

"I'm a little, um, grimy," he told her, but she grasped his hand anyway.

"I'm a little grimy, sometimes, too," she told him. "You came by it honestly. I owe you my life and my child's life. Thank you." And she went down the line, shaking the hand of each and every man.

"You got good taste in ladies, Lightning," Rip said as the men prepared to leave. "We'll see you when we see you." And the men slipped away.

Seth stood looking down at her. He reached out and touched her cheek, then cupped his hand around her jaw. "He didn't hurt you?"

She shook her head. "I might have hurt one or two of them. You taught me well." She laughed, but Seth didn't laugh back.

"I wanted to kill him," he told her.

"You're not that kind of man."

"Don't be so sure."

"I'm sure. And I'm safe, Seth. Thanks to you, I'm safe." She turned her head and kissed his palm.

She felt a shiver rip through his body. "We need to get you home."

"All right. And then we need to talk, Seth. Or should I call you Lightning?"

* * *

Seth couldn't stop looking at Molly as they walked. He wanted to reach out, to touch her, to feel that she was safe. But the question she had asked stopped him. It was a barrier and one he needed to respect.

"There's one thing I don't completely understand," she said. "How did you know that I was in trouble? How did you get there in time?" Her words grew weak on the last two words, and he threw caution to the wind, stopping, pulling her into his arms. He ran his hands down her back, just loving the solid feel of her flesh. She was unhurt. Her well-being was a blessing.

Seth took both of her hands in his. He leaned forward and kissed the top of her head. "I've been spying on you," he confessed, murmuring the words against her hair.

She went rigid, pulling back to stare up at him. "Oh, yes, you're a reporter," she said quietly. "I know."

He winced. "How? When?"

"Just today, and I'd rather not say how I know."

Seth frowned at that. "You hate reporters," he reminded her. "I want you to know that I didn't keep it a secret because I wanted to lie to you."

She visibly swallowed. "I know why you kept it a secret. I know about 'Mean Streets.' I suppose that's how you know Rip."

"Rip's a good man."

"I know that, too. I—Ada didn't tell you who I am, did she?"

"No, and you don't need to, either. I know all I need to know. If I spied on you it wasn't to find out your secrets, but only because I was worried that someone was trying to hurt you."

"He was," she said, and then she told him why. She told him about her childhood and why she had been on the run. "Kevin wanted to imprison Ruthie, to take her life away, to make her star power the only thing important about her. I couldn't let him do that. It's too difficult to be a child and to grow up knowing that the only thing your parents care about is how much money you can make for them."

Seth dropped a soft kiss on her downturned lips. "That would never happen with Ruthie. She has you."

"But if Kevin took her away…"

"He can't."

"Because you spied on me and brought the 'Mean Streets' gang to help." She rose on her toes and kissed him. "I have a secret to tell you."

"Another one?"

Molly nodded. "You know how I never wanted anyone interfering in my life, how I always want to be independent?"

"You're very good at being independent. Dom and Kevin will both bear some great bruises from those shoes you're wearing."

"They will, won't they?" she said with a little smile. "Well, I do have a confession to make. I've been interfering in your life. I went to see your sister today."

For a minute his chest felt as if it were going to implode. He could barely breathe. Then he carefully took her hand and started walking.

"Did you now?" he asked, and he didn't say anything more about that. He couldn't. He knew what she was doing. The amount of caring that it must have taken to do what she had done, well, it humbled him, but he couldn't go there.

"You won't have to worry about Kevin anymore, beyond having to appear in court to testify. Those guys he hired aren't the loyal type. They'll talk to save their own necks. I can't promise to keep the story out of the paper. There were too many people there for it not to leak out, but I promise you it will be covered fairly. Not by me, of course. I'm a bit too close to the story."

Shannon touched his arm. "Seth, did you hear me? I went to see Shannon."

"I heard you. Of course I can't make any promises about how the *Sentinel* will report the story. As a rival paper, I can't pull any strings there."

Molly sighed. She opened her mouth, then closed it again.

"Give it up, Molly," he told her.

She gave a small nod. "I wouldn't worry about the rival paper. I know a reporter for the *Sentinel*. I think I'll give Jeff an exclusive interview if the *Sentinel* agrees that his is the only story on me it will run."

"Jeff?" Something hard and ugly tugged at Seth. No question, it was jealousy. Also no question, he was going to ignore it. He didn't have the right to dictate who her friends and lovers were. And now that her world had been made safe...

"I assume you'll go back to your own world now that Kevin is in custody?" He tried very hard not to sound too interested.

Molly's heart felt scraped and raw at Seth's question. Of course, things were over. He had never intended to get involved with her. They lived such different lives, and he didn't want a relationship. It would be best for him if she left.

She struggled to speak, but it took a few seconds. "That would be best," she finally managed to say. She didn't close her eyes against the pain; she held to it. She didn't turn away from looking at him; she looked more, hoping to always remember.

"What—what will happen to your column now that your cover has been blown?"

Seth shrugged. "I may have to lie low for a while, but this is Chicago. There's always another pocket of the city to cover, another apartment to move to if I need to. If I have to, I'll take an alias and continue my work."

And you'll be alone, she thought. Always alone. It was his choice, of course, but she loved him, and so it hurt.

Get over it, she told herself, but her heart didn't listen.

"We'd better go get Ruthie," he said, his voice rough

edged. He took her elbow and guided her down the street. She leaned into him. For a short time longer, she could pretend it wasn't over.

Chapter 20

"When will you leave?" Seth asked when Molly had
told Ada what had happened, said her goodbyes, gathered up Ruthie and allowed him to take her home.

Molly looked around the tiny apartment that she had
tried to make a home, the place where Seth had coached
her, made love to her, taught her how to fend for herself.

If I don't think about never seeing him again, I'll be
all right, she thought, but she knew she lied.

Instead, she tried to concentrate on what would happen to Seth after she had gone. She didn't want him to
be alone.

"I think Shannon needs you," she said.

Seth's eyes closed for a second. When he opened

them again, they were filled with pain. "I've learned your secrets. Let me tell you mine. Let me tell you about Shannon." And she knew he was doing what he had never done before. Sharing the story that had broken his heart.

He pulled her down beside him on the couch and looked into her eyes. "When I became Shannon's guardian, I was petrified. I didn't know a thing about being a parent, and I was so afraid that I would lose her, too. So I made rules, lots of rules, tons of rules, and she hated every one of them."

Molly shook her head. "She was a young girl, Seth. That's natural."

"Yes, but only up to a point, because I had a rule for everything. I knew what I was doing wasn't working, but I just kept doing it. I thought that if I controlled every minute of her day, I could keep her safe. I believed that right up until the day she ran away."

He paused, his voice growing rough. Molly reached out, but he stopped her with a look. "No, let me finish."

She waited.

"On the streets—"

"I know. She told me."

"She told you she was raped?"

Molly sucked in a breath. "She intimated that bad things happened to her."

Seth gave a harsh laugh. "She was beaten badly while she was pregnant, she had a miscarriage, and now she can never have another child. I never met a little girl who wanted babies more than Shannon did when she was growing up."

Seth's gaze grew hard, anguished.

Molly couldn't help herself then. She rose to her knees, leaned forward and wrapped her arms around Seth. She kissed him.

He sat rigid at first. She knew he was denying himself because of the renewed guilt that she had stirred up with her prodding, but still she held on. She kissed him again.

"She still loves you," she said quietly.

He pulled back, staring directly into her eyes. "You amaze me," he said, and then he kissed her. He leaned her back and took everything she was offering.

"I need you today," he said.

"I need you, too."

"I don't want to hurt you," Seth whispered. "If I'm going to hurt you by making love to you again, tell me to leave now."

She knew what he meant. She could hear it in his voice when he talked about Shannon. His sister would never have the joys of children and a family. Consequently, Molly knew he would never allow himself to have those things, either. How could he pursue his own happiness when he felt he had been instrumental in robbing his sister of hers?

"Molly?" he asked, bracing himself on his elbows, a mere breath away from her lips.

"Don't leave," she whispered, and she reached for

him. It would only be this one last time, she knew. She couldn't ask him to stay with her forever, but today… just today…she would take what he was offering.

Seth made slow, sweet love to her, rising to kiss her as he stripped away her clothing, savoring each part of her. He kissed every square inch of her and then, and only then, he removed his shirt.

"Seth," she whispered, looking at his beautiful, scarred body.

"Let's make it last," he said.

"Yes." It was all she could say. Slowly she removed his pants, the black boxers that hid him from view.

When he lowered himself to her, he entered her slowly and with his eyes open, gazing into her own.

"I'm never going to forget you," he told her. "I'm never going to be the same now that I've known you."

She fought to hold back the tears. If he ever knew how much she loved him, how much it hurt to leave him—well, she refused to be another woman on his conscience.

She refused to cry. She allowed herself only the here and now. She told him the truth, or at least all of the truth that she could give him without hurting him. "You were good for us," she said. "So very good. You've made my life and my world so much better."

Then he joined his body to hers. He moved in her slowly. When they went over the edge, she touched the stars…and knew she would probably never again know love this deep or fulfilling. And yet she was glad that

she had at least had the opportunity to know and love
Seth McCabe one long winter.

When Seth woke, Molly was closing the zipper on
her suitcase. She looked at him sadly.

"It's time," she said. "I need to take Ruthie home to
claim what's hers. I have to get my life in order."

Somewhere else, he thought, his chest tightening at
the thought. "Do you need—what can I get for you?"

She shook her head. "Now that you've taken Kevin
off the streets, I don't have to hide or run anymore. I can
use my accounts, and I do have them. You know the
truth about me, don't you?"

He knew she had once been known nationwide. "I
suppose you're a wealthy woman." He swung his legs
off the couch and pulled his jeans on. "That doesn't
mean a thing to me. I'll take you where you need to go."

For a moment she looked as if she might say yes. He
half hoped she would and half hoped she wouldn't.
Saying goodbye to her was killing him, but the thought
of having her gone…

"No," she finally said softly. "I want to say goodbye
here, where we knew each other. I've already called a
cab."

Something painful sliced through him. He thrust it
aside. "All right then. We end here." He finished
dressing and then he waited while she picked up
Ruthie.

"So long, princess," he said, rubbing one lean finger

gently over the baby's cheek. Ruthie surprised him and Molly by grasping it.

I was there the night you came into the world, munchkin, he thought. *Have a good, happy life.* He wished he could see her grow up.

"She'll break hearts," was all he said. "Come on, let's get you gone." And he took her bags and led her out the door onto the street to where the cab was already waiting.

He placed the bags into the cab, then turned to Molly, wanting to tell her all that was in his heart, that she *was* his heart, that he loved her, but knowing that just wouldn't be fair. Because he was never going to offer forever, and she was a woman who would need and had the right to expect forever. He wanted to beg her to stay, to tell her he could be something other than who and what he was, but she had already been hurt badly by a lying snake. She didn't need any more liars in her life. "You'll be all right?" he somehow managed to say.

She nodded, but her eyes told him that this moment was distressing her as much as it was him. He cursed himself for not being able to make this easier for her. He needed her to end this cleanly. But...

"Mind if I ask where you're going?" he asked.

She shrugged. "Iowa. Aragon. Not real big. It's where my aunt raised me. You've probably never heard of it."

"I have now," he said, knowing the name would be forever emblazoned on his brain. And he was likely to do stupid things like research the town on the Internet, like lying awake at night imagining her there, like taking the long route to avoid the town if he should ever pass that way. Because once she was gone, he could never trust himself to see her again. Doing this once was hard enough. Doing it again? Impossible.

But he couldn't say any of that. Instead he leaned forward and allowed himself to touch her just once more. He kissed her, ever so gently. He breathed her in one last time. "Take care of yourself, Molly. And watch out for those reporters. If any of them trail you this time, just tell them to go to hell. You've done your time with reporters." He gave her a grin as he said it, but in the end it wasn't funny. He watched her struggle to return the smile.

"You're not bad for a reporter," she told him. "Goodbye, Seth." And she gave him a quick, hard kiss and turned to place Ruthie into the car seat in the cab. When she was done, she climbed inside and looked up at him without saying another word.

He watched the cab until it was just a yellow speck on the road. It was time to move on.

But still he watched and waited.

Molly struggled not to let her tears fall. "We're going, hon," she whispered to Ruthie. "And we're never coming back. I wish you had been old enough to actually know him. I wish—"

She wished a great many things, almost all of them

impossible. Only one seemed to hold out any hope. She couldn't have Seth, ever, but...

"I need to make one stop on the way to the train," she told the driver. "Will you wait?"

"You pay me for the time I'm sitting still, I'll wait," he told her. She gave him the address.

Just a short time later, she and Ruthie got out in front of Shannon's house and told the driver it might be a while. She rang the doorbell and, eventually, a sleepy-eyed Shannon let her into the building and the apartment.

"My, you're an early riser, aren't you?" Shannon asked.

Molly shrugged. "I'm on my way out of town."

Shannon fixed her with a stare. "My brother have anything to do with this?"

"He saved my life yesterday. Gave me my future back. That's all." But she couldn't look Shannon directly in the eye.

"I see. He saved you, and so you pay him back by running."

"It's not like that between Seth and me," Molly protested. "It was never meant to be forever."

"He isn't good enough for you?"

Molly raised her chin and this time she stared directly at Shannon. "You know there's not a better man around. We just...forever was never a possibility."

"But you care about him."

"I care. That's why I'm here. You told me that he

helped you when you first came back to Chicago. Now he needs *your* help."

"He say that?"

"*I'm* saying that."

"That's not the same, and you know it."

She did, but she hadn't been able to leave without at least trying.

At that moment a door opened behind Shannon and Jeff Payton walked into the room rubbing a towel on his wet hair. He grinned at Molly, an infectious, boyish grin. Sad as she was, she couldn't help smiling back, especially because Shannon, tough little Shannon, was actually blushing.

Molly decided to let her save face. "Jeff, I'm glad you're here," she said. "I was going to call you anyway."

"You were? What for?" Shannon asked, a trace of jealousy in her tone.

"Shannon," Molly drawled. "I don't even know Jeff. This is business. I have a story I want him to write."

Jeff raised a brow. "Tell me more," he said, and Molly sat him down and told him who she was and what she had become. She quickly related everything that had happened to her these past few weeks. Well, almost everything. She left out the part about falling in love with Seth.

"I don't want Seth's name included, of course," she said, "but the rest of the story is yours if you want it. I've spent most of my life running from the press. I don't want to run anymore. I want to show my daughter how to face life head-on, and I can't do that if I'm always hiding. I'm pretty sure that I can count on you to be fair."

Jeff stepped forward and took Molly's hand. "I promise you that I will. Thank you. You don't know what this means to me. It means I can begin to think about having a future." He looked toward Shannon, and it was clear to Molly that he meant the whole deal, a forever kind of deal.

Shannon fidgeted and blushed again. "Forget it. I'm not your type," she said.

"You were my type last night."

"That was just sex."

He frowned. "It wasn't, for either of us, and don't tell me it was."

Hugging herself, Shannon paced. "I'm bad, I have bad habits, lots of them," she said. "Not like you."

Jeff looked at her with love. "I like bad girls," he said.

"Well, tough. I'm bad, but I'm not stupid. I know temporary when I see it."

"Shannon," he said, "you are never going to be a temporary anything with me. I loved you on sight. I love you whether you're good, bad or indifferent. I just love…you."

A small cry escaped her. "Molly, tell him. Tell him why he's an idiot for saying such things, why I can't be with him."

"Can't see a reason," Molly said.

"Well, then, you're just as blind as he is. Just look at

him. He's Mr. Clean-cut, Mr. Family Man. I can't—Jeff, I can't have any children." Her last words were merely a tortured whisper.

"That's not a problem, then, because I'm not a child, Shannon," he said gently. "I'm house-trained, too, and furthermore, I think you're the most beautiful, interesting, fascinating, wonderful woman I've ever met."

Shannon stood there as if she wanted to run, but she couldn't decide whether to run to Jeff or away from him.

Molly stood up, figuring the two of them needed some privacy. She went to Shannon and hugged her. "I have to go now, but I'll be in touch. I know you're brave. Now, be smart, as well."

Shannon nodded and hugged her back. "You sure you can't stay?"

Molly shook her head. "It would hurt too much." It was already hurting too much, she thought as she walked away, and this time the tears flowed. She placed Ruthie in the cab, signaled the driver and rode away from all that she had come to love.

"Just you and me now, sweetie," she told her child. It would have to be enough.

Chapter 21

Seth answered the fierce knocking on his door. He stared blurry eyed down at an angry Ada.

"Something wrong, Ada?" he asked, rubbing his stubbled jaw.

"Other than the fact that I haven't heard your footsteps in the hallway even once in the past few days, or the fact that you look like you haven't been eating, sleeping or working? I'd say yes, there's something wrong. You're acting like an idiot, and you never were one before."

He looked to the side.

"You miss her. You should go see her."

He scowled. "You know I'm not doing that."

She planted her hands on her hips. "Well, do something. You need a distraction. You're making me... scared." And the quivery tone in her aging voice finally got his attention.

Seth ran a hand back through his hair. "All right then," he said. "I'll get out of the house and get some fresh air. Will that work for you?"

"You going to see Molly?"

"I'm going out, Ada. Don't ask for more."

"All right, then. I know when to stop pushing." She left him to take care of things on his own. Forty-five minutes later, he stepped out into sunlight, trying not to remember how Molly's hair had looked when the sun hit it. He did his best not to think of her at all. Mostly he just walked.

And surprised himself by finding himself in front of his sister's apartment. What had Molly told him? That Shannon loved him, that she needed him?

He doubted that; still Molly wasn't a liar. "Just misinformed," he muttered, knocking on the door.

When Shannon answered it, he couldn't speak for a minute. He just stared. She stared, too. And then, silently, she pulled the door open farther, ushering him in.

"Hi, Seth. Did Molly send you?" she asked.

Seth's heart clenched at the sound of Molly's name. "I haven't seen her in two weeks," he confessed. To his chagrin, he sounded as bad as he felt.

"She's okay," Shannon said. "She called me."

He knew she was okay. Molly had called Ada, as well. Everyone but him.

But he knew that it had taken a lot for Shannon to say something nice to him. "Thank you," he said. "How—how are you?"

"Better than you, I'd say," she answered with a smile. And for the first time in two weeks, he smiled, too.

"You're probably right. It's good to see you."

"Likewise, big brother." Shannon's voice was soft, softer than he remembered. But then, mostly he remembered the fighting and the resentment. He decided to take a chance.

"I've missed you," he told her.

And then a tear slid down her cheek.

"Aw, damn," he said.

"I'm fine." Shannon's voice choked as she hurriedly swiped at her eyes.

"I'm not. Shannon, I'm just…not." Seth stepped forward and tugged Shannon into his arms. He hugged her the way he hadn't for many long years.

"Seth. Oh, Seth, I'm so sorry."

"You've got nothing to be sorry for. I do."

"You don't. I was always such a brat."

"You were a person, a young lady. I didn't treat you like one. I treated you like a baby."

"You were just protecting me. I guess I knew that. Molly said so, too, though, when we talked."

At the mention of Molly's name, Seth's heart finished breaking. It had been torn badly, but he had been trying to hold it together. Now, knowing how hard she had worked to get him and Shannon back together, that she *had* gotten them back together, he couldn't beat back the pain of losing her.

"I should have been here sooner, years ago," he said.

"You were. Mrs. K. told me you came by. Besides, I didn't make it easy for you, what with sending your checks back torn in half."

"You hated me."

"No! No, I just…was ashamed of all that I'd done and said and become."

He touched her face. "You never changed in my mind. You're still Little Freckleface." He called her by his pet childhood name.

She grinned. "Call me that again, and I'll get Jeff to give you a pounding."

He did a double take at that. "Jeff?"

She blushed. "My boyfriend. He's in the other room. He's a reporter doing Molly's story."

Seth bristled at that. "A reporter?"

Shannon laughed. "Ah, you don't like the species? How precious, when you're one of the best."

"Only one of the best?"

"Well, there's Jeff, you know." She looked over her shoulder toward the other room. "I'll introduce you soon." It was clear as anything that she was in love. How could he object? He could.

"He'd better treat you right."

"He treats me like a princess. He tries to protect me. Reminds me of someone else I know in that respect."

"Hmm, maybe he's not so bad then," Seth said with a grin.

"No, he's not so bad, Seth. He's wonderful. I love him. It scares me sometime to realize how much I love him. You know?" Her voice was slightly scared.

He knew. Pain zigzagged through him. He nodded slowly.

"You love her, too, don't you? I can tell that you're not happy."

"I'm happy," he protested. "I'm talking to you for the first time in years. I'm blessed. You know?" he asked, echoing her words.

She nodded and swiped at a new tear. "I know exactly what you mean, but…you love her. You should be with her. I would be even happier than I am right now if you had Molly, too. I could swear she cared for you, too. When she left…" It was a question rather than a statement.

"I didn't try to stop her," he said, supplying the answer.

"Why not?"

He held out his hands helplessly. "It's complicated. Shannon, I'm more glad than I can say that you let me in the door, that I'm here looking at you, that you want to still be my sister, but you don't know how it was. I— when you were growing up, I was responsible for your welfare, damn it! I drove you away. I let you get hurt, raped, beaten, caught in the clutches of some street thug. I was the worst kind of parent, Shannon, controlling, clueless, useless in the end. When I think of what you went through out there alone…how could I ever do that to a child again? Molly has a baby. How could I ever ask her to trust me to be a father to her child?"

Shannon listened until the end of his speech and then she grabbed him by the shirtfront. "You listen to me, Seth McCabe. You're my brother and I never stopped loving you, even when I was calling you a lot of filthy names and telling you how much I hated you. I can't tell you how grateful I am that you rang my doorbell this morning, and I know that has to be partly Molly's doing. I'm grateful to her for getting me my brother back, and I don't ever want to lose you again, you hear, but…"

She leaned back and looked at him, biting her lip as tears streamed down her face.

"You're giving her up for some silly, noble reason," she said, her voice soft and incredibly sad.

"You were hurt," he reminded her.

"I was almost destroyed," she agreed, "but that wasn't your doing. Don't you know what you did for me all those years?"

"I tried to control you. I ruled with an iron will."

"Okay, you went a little overboard with the rules. Show me one parent who probably doesn't do that now and then. It's a tough job, but you did the best you could. Hell, Seth, you were only nineteen when Mom and Dad died. And yes, I resented you for trying to be a parent when I had lost mine. And when I ended up on the street and messed up so badly, I was ashamed because I didn't want you to find out. But you were what gave me the will to go on when I lost Mom and Dad. The thought of you being alive was what kept *me* alive and intent on doing everything I could to get back home. You were the person I looked up to—you gave me a reason to keep trying. It was the mistakes you made because you loved me that kept me loving you, not your attempts to be perfect. Stop trying to keep your emotions in check, Seth. Stop trying to be so damned invincible. Make mistakes. You don't have to keep being the perfect parent. Just be you. Just be my brother, the one I loved and, yes, hated at times. Be my brother who needs to love and be loved, who needs to forgive and be forgiven, just like Molly told me you did."

Tears threatened to blind Seth. He caught his sister in his arms. "Thank you, Shannon," he whispered against her temple.

"For what?"

"For your words, for my memories of you, for just…staying alive."

"Oh, that." She gave him a teary smile and kissed him on the cheek.

"That's a hell of a lot," he told her. "You're most likely right about the fact that I've tried to be too perfect. I've blamed myself for a lot, but mostly for not being Dad, for not being able to save him and Mom."

"You've done a lot of good," she reminded him, "and not just for me. Jeff tells me your column really makes a difference in people's lives."

He shrugged.

"Say it," she said.

"Say what?"

"Say something good about yourself."

He chuckled. "I suppose my column has helped a few people take note of some problems they might otherwise have ignored."

"It's a start," she said with a sigh. "A pitiful start, but a start nonetheless. Now tell me that you deserve Molly."

He shook his head with a sad smile. "I'll never deserve Molly and Ruthie."

She frowned and opened her mouth.

He held up a hand to let her know he wasn't finished. "I don't deserve them, but I love them," he conceded. "Beyond belief."

"So tell them, Seth. Let them know. And then, please, bring them here, bring them home. I want all of you here for my wedding."

"A wedding? Hey, am I even going to get to meet the groom before this happy event?" He tried to look like the old Seth, stern and stormy.

She pinched him and wrinkled her nose. "You'll meet him soon enough. Just go get Molly. Be happy, Seth."

And suddenly he realized the import of this day. He had found the sister who had been lost to him for years, and he'd found her through Molly. His love for Molly soared. He missed her like mad. And he wanted her…right now.

A slow smile lifted his lips.

"You're going to do it, aren't you?" Shannon asked with a smile.

He looked down at her and tweaked her nose. "I'm going to try. If it's not too late."

Molly pushed her grocery cart out to her car. "Look at this, sweetie," she told Ruthie, who was in a carrier in the cart. "You and mom are buying groceries *and* we have our own car, which we will take home to our own pretty little house. We don't have to look over our shoulders. We don't have to worry about a thing. How cool is that?"

Ruthie smiled at her mother's tone, but Molly knew that her words had been a bit forced. She felt guilty about that. Everything she had said was true, so why wasn't she happier?

"Darn him," she muttered.

A lady pushing her cart nearby chuckled. "It's always a man who makes a woman miserable, isn't it?"

Oh, but he hadn't made her miserable. He had brought her joy. It was not having him around at all that was messing her up so badly.

Get used to it, she told herself. Forget him.

She was trying, so very hard, but it was as if she saw him everywhere. If she saw a tall, dark-haired man in the distance, her heart did a flip-flop until she was close enough to realize that he didn't look a bit like Seth. If she picked up a newspaper, she thought of him. When she went to her new self-defense class, she remembered how he had looked when he had taught her to protect herself.

He was in her thoughts far more than was wise. She had already stupidly stopped total strangers on the street and then had to stammer an apology. So when she looked up and saw Seth walking toward her through the parking lot, she did her best to ignore her idiotic erratic heartbeat. She continued moving toward her car.

"Molly," the man said, just the way the real Seth would have.

She stumbled slightly and looked up again, assuming the miragelike Seth would have disappeared.

But he hadn't.

"Seth?" Her voice quivered.

He smiled at her, the smile she remembered so well. Tears of joy ran through her soul. "Where did you come from?"

He nodded toward a bright blue minivan, a family car. How strange. Of course, Seth with any car was an oddity. The Seth she knew didn't even own one.

"Hey, Ruthie girl," he said, grinning down at the baby and brushing his finger gently over her cheek. "You're just as cute as ever, I see. Gonna knock all the boys dead someday."

Ruthie burbled.

Seth winked at her.

Molly blinked. Had Seth, her Seth, her somber Seth actually winked?

She looked up to find a gorgeous smile transforming his face. For a moment she wanted to stand there and stare at him forever.

"Why...I don't understand. Why are you here?"

He cocked his head. "Maybe because I heard that a former famous star was in town, or maybe just because I heard that the most beautiful woman in the world had moved in. I'm a reporter, remember? I hear things. Care to tell me the story about what you've been doing these past two weeks, beautiful?"

Molly's heart soared. Seth was smiling. He was happy in a way she hadn't seen him happy before.

"Something's happened," she said. "Something good."

"Ah, my sweet and wise Molly. You're so right. Shannon and I had a long talk yesterday. I have my sister back, thanks to you."

"And you came here to tell me that. That's wonderful news. I'm so glad," she said, understanding now. He had come to share his news. This was just a quick pass through. She tried very hard not to show her disappointment.

"I wanted you to know, and yes, I wanted to thank you with all my heart, but that's not why I'm here."

"I don't understand then. Are you...did your newspaper send you?"

And then he did something wonderful. He reached out and cupped her jaw. He stroked his thumb over her lips. "I wouldn't come here for that. Remember what I told you to tell any reporters you met?"

She managed to nod, even though doing so only made his touch more intimate, made her long for more. "You told me to tell them to go to hell."

He studied her carefully. "I noticed you haven't done that yet." He waited.

She tried to speak, but all she could think was that Seth was here and they were talking like old friends. Friends, not lovers.

"I could never tell you that," she said. "You know that."

He touched her again, his fingers brushing across her lips. It was all she could do not to beg him to kiss her. "Good," he said, his own voice husky, "because I've already been to hell any number of times and heaven is so much better. Have you ever been to heaven, Molly?"

Of course she had. Every time she had been in Seth's arms it had been heaven. "I might have," she said, her voice coming out on a whisper.

"That's good." Seth nodded.

Now she was really getting worried, because, while Seth was still smiling, she could see a definite hint of stress in his eyes. What had Shannon and Ada told him about their conversations with her?

"Seth, are you here because you're worried about me? Because if you are, I want you to know that you don't have to be. You worry too much, you take care of too many people."

"And you don't?" He studied her closely.

"I…"

"You ran errands for Ada and cleaned her place. You cooked for me, you brought me together with my sister, and you convinced Shannon to give Jeff a chance."

She could think of no way to answer that. "I shouldn't have interfered with your sister," she finally said.

"Why not? She's happy now. I'm happy now."

Which was wonderful. She wanted him to be happy. It was just that she was so…unhappy that the contrast made her heart hurt.

"I'm glad you're happy," she whispered.

"You're not smiling," he told her.

She tried to smile, and then he frowned. "Molly, you wish I hadn't come, don't you? Just tell me this, am I too late? Is there someone else? Someone you've met in the past two weeks? Maybe someone you loved before you came to Chicago? Some man you prefer to me?"

"You think I slept with you when I was in love with another man? What kind of woman do you think I am?"

"A wonderful one, but…"

"There's no one else," she said. "Of course I haven't found someone else I prefer. I will never find someone like you, and that's why I'm so upset. It's such a waste."

"What is?" he asked.

"All this…all this love," she whispered.

Seth tugged her into his arms. He closed his eyes and kissed her temple. "I swear it's not a waste, Molly. Your love? Never. So, love me, Molly. Please love me, because heaven knows I don't want to live without you anymore. I've been half-insane without you. I've missed you, I love you. Stay with me."

His lips came down on hers and she wrapped her arms around his neck, tears gathering in her eyes.

"Shh, don't cry," he said, kissing her eyelids.

"I can't help it. I've ached for you so much, and when you showed up, for a moment I was sure you were a mirage. I've seen you in my dreams so many times in the past two weeks."

He pulled her hand to his chest, where she felt his thudding heartbeat. "No mirage, just a man."

"My man," she said.

"Always. Will you marry me, Molly, you and Ruthie?"

"Any time you're ready."

He smiled and kissed her again. "I'm ready right now. Come home with me, Molly? I'm thinking of buying a pretty little house with new locks."

"And no nosy reporters?" she teased.

"Maybe just one."

Molly smiled and leaned close to Seth's ear. "I know just which reporter I want to tell all my secrets to."

And her great brooding, scarred hero threw back his head and laughed. "Thank you for falling into my life, Molly Delavan."

"Thank you for finding me, Seth McCabe."

"Luckiest day of my life. Maybe ours really is a match made in heaven."

"Or Chicago," she teased.

"You mean Chicago isn't heaven?"

She smiled, snaked her arms around his neck and kissed him for a good long time. "It is when you're there," she whispered against his mouth.

"Then by all means, let me take you to heaven, love," he said. And together they gathered up their child and went back to the beautiful Mean Streets to live out their life together.

* * * * *

Maybe this time they'll make it down the aisle

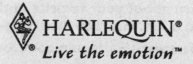